THE SOUND OF HORROR

2007

First Edition
ISBN 10 0-9797000-0-0
ISBN 13 978-0-9797000-0-2

Magus Press
743 N. Lafayette
Salt Lake City, UT 84116
United States
http://www.MagusPress.com

Table of Contents

Introduction:
An Interview With Michael Laimo

Michael Laimo is the author of over one hundred short stories and several novels. He's was nominated for the Bram Stoker Award for Best First Novel. His short story "Anxiety" is being made into a movie as well as his novel Deep in the Darkness.

Magus: *Sound plays a large role in horror movies. What role do you think sound plays in horror literature?*

Laimo: Absolutely. It is a very important part of creating atmosphere in horror writing. Not to be overdone, a simple descriptive passage utilizing a sense of sound can intensify a scene. Is it quiet? Noisy? Is there only one sound? Or two? Depending on the scene you write, exploring the sense of sound to the character's ears is a crucial and imperative part in successful scene-setting. For instance, if your character enters an old house in the middle of the night, a writer must take time to not only explore what this character might be seeing and feeling, but also hearing as well. Does the door creak when he enters? Does it slam shut behind him? Do his footsteps creak? Does a bird flutter in the rafters? Does the wind rattle the windowpanes? I could go on and on...

One scene that sticks with me from Dead Souls involves the sound of a hanging body, swinging, tapping against the wall. How do you utilize sound in your own work?

Well, as mentioned, I take sound very seriously and utilize where I see fit, without overdoing it. A writer could go on and on in an effort to describe what is being heard, so it is important to reveal only what is necessary as to not bog down the prose. With that scene, sound is cricual because it is what propels the scene forward. A strange sound hitting against the wall from the next room? That's something that must be investigated. I used that same exact concept for short story, Room 412. I liked it so much, I reused it in Dead Souls.

Are there any example of an author that you feel

uses sound particularly well in his or her novels?

Off the top of my head, King did it quite well in IT, especially the bathroom scene with the blood gurgling up form the sink. Clive Barker is another author that utilizes a good sense of sound description. In Coldheart Canyon, the sounds of the ghosts in the woods outside the house was brilliantly executed.

Magus: *Does horror have a sound or sounds?*

Laimo: No one sound in particular is 'horror'. Certain sounds are associated with the horror genre, like those classic tones used in slasher films (eee, eee, eee!), and haunted house organ music, for example. But anything can seem horror in nature when used in the right context. The remake of Dawn of the Dead made Heavy Metal music (Disturbed) scary, and Eyes Wide Shut made chant scary

Magus: *Is there a particular sound that haunts you?*

Laimo: Yes! Low grinding sounds get to me. Like

that used while the zombies were feasting in Night of the Living Dead. Gives me the creeps just thinking about it.

Magus: *Is there anything that you dread to hear?*

Yeah, my kids crying in the middle of the night. Can't they just get up and get their own drinks? LOL, really, in movies and literature, nothing really unnerves me, but I really dread hearing sirens in the city because behind every one of them, there's someone in distress. I find that saddening.

Magus: *What do you think is unique about short stories as opposed to novels?*

Laimo: Short fiction is a challenge, and for me it relies more on tight plotting, and description, rather than characterization, unless your story exceeds 5000 words. Then there some room to explore deeper into your character's psyche. Short fiction is a quick fix, like a one night stand with a stranger. A novel is a relationship with a special person, one that entertains both the physical and mental aspects of a courtship. Short fiction was a great way for me to hone my craft, to find my voice so to speak. There was a great deal of trial and error, resulting in some very bad stories. But every now and then a gem would come out of me, and give me the motivation to carry on. These few good stories ended up in my collection, Demons, Freaks and Other Abnormalities.

Magus: *What turned you onto horror?*

Laimo: Ever since I was a little kid, I've been drawn to all things dark and mysterious. I used to read all the true-account ghost story books in the library at a very young age. And it's stayed with me ever since, but just in alternative forms, from reading books to watching movies to eventually trying to write scary stuff myself. I do also like to read fantasy, mystery, and science fiction, but horror is my main love.

Magus: *When you sit down to write, what is it you like to hear?*

Laimo: Primarily, I enjoy the ambience of the environment I'm in, whether it be the quiet hum of the train I'm in, or the chatter of the café. I can write to music, but there must not be any vocals, otherwise I start humming the words and it gets distracting. I like ambient, techno, and even classical when writing.

Magus: *I always tell people to never start a publishing company. Do you have anything cautionary to say to the people out there?*

Laimo: Well, I've never done any of my own publishing, though I did work as an associate editor in the past for Space & Time, and edited the horror antho Bloodtype. The time that went into the editing alone was heavy, so I could not imagine having to start up my own publishing company. I spend too much time writing, and do not want to take away from that.

Mr. Creator

By Joe McKinney

"Well," said Miles Fesler, my new landlord, "this is it. Fifty dollars a month. Just like we discussed."

He was an obscenely fat, grizzled man in his late fifties with a horse-like face and eyes that reminded me of jaundice, a sickly yellow. We'd walked up three flights of stairs to get to the apartment and it'd left him winded. He wheezed wetly while he talked.

I glanced around at my new accommodations and sighed. The room was a depressingly small box with two yellowed windows on the north wall. I went over to them and looked out at Cattleman's Square, a rectangular field of poorly manicured grass in the midst of moldering urban decay and poverty that gave the area its name. Tenement buildings shouldered up against the Square on three sides, and I could hear the delighted screams of children, squawking mothers, and the not so distant traffic noises of the city at twilight.

The San Antonio skyline loomed beyond the tenements, and the sky was a charcoal smear of black, foul smog against a rust-colored sunset. It was strangely beautiful, not without a certain romantic charm, but as I turned back to the apartment I had to admit that there was little romance to poverty when seen from close up. The wood floor was badly scuffed, the plaster on the walls was flaking off in great leprous chunks, and there were several suspicious stains. A fine patina of dust covered everything and a large brown cockroach stared up at me brazenly from a corner near the back wall. The only light came from a naked bulb hanging by a string in the center of the room.

"There's no bathroom," I said, wrinkling my nose at the lingering odor of mold that seemed to come from everywhere at once.

Fesler wiped the sweat from the back of his hairy neck with a gray snot rag. "Yeah," he said, still wheezing, "the best thing for that is a bucket."

I gawked at him. "A bucket?"

He nodded without a trace of apology. "That's what the other tenants do. I own the hardware store down on the first floor. If you want I can sell you one."

I studied the man, trying to find some indication that he was joking, but apparently he wasn't.

"You *are* getting the place cheap," he said.

Yeah, cheap, I thought. I had exactly $371.14 in my pocket, which in my estimation made the word *cheap* dangerously suggestive.

But I didn't have any other choice. I'd thoroughly wrecked a marriage, lost a job, and alienated my two teenage sons. This was rock bottom, and it was either build myself back up from here or die in the dust with the roaches.

And I still had a little will to live.

I put my painting supplies down in the middle of the room, and with the air of a man accepting a lengthy prison sentence, said, "Fine. I'll take it."

Fesler nodded. I don't think he doubted I'd say anything else.

"Are my neighbors quiet?" I said. "I like quiet."

"You've only got the one on this floor," he said. "His name's Wesley Suffles. Good man. Folks around the Square think the world of him."

Fesler suddenly smiled brightly, an unsettling,

black-toothed gesture that made my stomach turn. "Say, I bet the two of you'll get on like a house on fire. He's a writer. Same as you."

"I'm a painter," I said patiently. "I do portraits mostly."

"Even better," he said. He clapped his hands together and waddled toward the door. "Rent's due first of the month. Come see me about the bucket if that's what you decide to do."

"Thanks," I said. "I'll do that."

-SOH-

Two hours later, after the sun went down and the sounds of playing children were gone from the Square, I went down to Fesler's hardware store and did just that. I also bought an ice chest--another of his recommendations. With two dollars worth of ice I could keep my food in it for four or five days without rotting.

On the way back from the convenience store on the corner, as I was climbing the stairs up to the third landing, I met my neighbor, Wesley Suffles.

I recalled Fesler's words, that everybody in the

Square thought the world of Suffles, though as I stared up at him, I strained at the hyperbole. He was at the top of the stairs, completely naked save for his gym socks, waving a bottle of tequila around with one hand and a ball point pen with the other, like some parody of a concert conductor.

He was so fat his gut, which was covered by coarse gray hair, hung over his genitalia, and for a moment I wondered if they even existed. His skin, where it wasn't hairy, was a pale road map of blue veins, and his doughy face was lit red with intoxication.

"Hello," I said, because nothing else seemed to answer to the situation.

Suffles blinked at me.

"I'm your new neighbor across the hall," I said.

"I know who you are," he said. His words were wet and slurred, like his tongue was too big for his mouth. "You're William Barton."

"That's right. I guess Mr. Fesler told you—"

"What are you doing here?"

I tried to smile. "Excuse me?"

"What are you doing here?" he demanded. He looked confused, angry. "What are you doing here?

Here? You're supposed to be in St. Louis murdering your wife."

The smile drained from my face and a tight-lipped scowl took its place. I was from St. Louis. I'd hated my wife so much I'd had to get away from her. And, yes, I'd even had fantasies about killing her. But of course I'd told no one about that. No one knew me in San Antonio. I was just a name on a lease in a rattrap apartment.

"You're drunk," I said.

"That's true," Suffles said, swaying dangerously on the top stair. "But you haven't told me what you're doing here. How can you be here?"

"We'll talk another time," I said stiffly. "When you're more...put together."

I walked up the stairs, past Suffles, who stared after me, seemingly unaware of his own nakedness.

I glanced back at him as I fumbled the key into the lock and then hurriedly went inside. With my back to the door, I listened for movement out on the landing, praying for the man to go away.

When at last he wandered off, I went to my painting supplies and set up a canvas. I had brought a mirror with me, but it had cracked on the bus ride down from St. Louis, so that now it looked like a car's windshield that's been hit with a brick.

Still, I thought, as I looked into my shattered reflection, it suits me.

And I began my first painting, a self-portrait.

-SOH-

I spent the next two weeks working on my sketchbook. Facial studies, mostly. I couldn't afford a live model, so I had to settle for taking mental snapshots of the people I met in the Square. Whenever I found an interesting subject, I'd quickly transfer his or her likeness to the sketchbook and then over the next few days I'd rework the original likeness into a portrait worth putting onto a canvas. It was a slow process, but I had plenty of time on my hands.

I enjoyed my work. For the first time in years, I was actually enjoying myself, and I can't tell you how liberating that felt. I was...well, I was free. I can't think of another way to describe it. It was glorious.

My only complaint was the shoddy quality of my surroundings. Oh, I don't mean the dirtiness of it.

No, that I expected, especially considering what I was paying for it. What got to me was the constant noise I heard from Wesley Suffles' apartment. It was a scratching noise, a steady, unnaturally loud, pen on paper scratching. You wouldn't think I'd be able to hear something like that through the wall--from a completely different apartment at that--but there it was just the same.

Constant.

Steady.

Scratch scratch scratch.

In the beginning, I dismissed it as an echo of my frayed nerves. So many people had picked and pulled on me for so many years, everybody wanting something, some quick piece of my time, that I almost felt *I* had ceased to exist. *Me time* had disappeared from my life.

Then I thought, *Brain tumor.* People with brain tumors hallucinate, don't they? See birds at the foot of their bed. Think the carpet they're walking on is beach sand.

And then I thought, Well, if it is a brain tumor, I guess I'm screwed. I don't have the money to do anything about it anyway, so just go on with life such as it is.

Ignore the scratching if you can.

And so I threw myself into my painting, and to my surprise, I enjoyed myself.

One day, as I was wandering the Square, I happened to see a young mother and her two sons. The older boy looked about five, the younger maybe three. The mother was busily shepherding the boys down the front stairs of one of the tenements, telling them over and over again that they'd miss it if they didn't hurry.

Though I was intrigued by what *it* was, I was more interested in their faces. The young woman had a black eye, the left one. Her shiny black hair was thick, but crudely styled, and fell about her face in clumps. She wasn't especially slender, but she was attractive, despite the black eye and the beleaguered look of worry that haunted her features.

It didn't seem to me that she was running from someone, as the black eye might have otherwise suggested, but rather that she was worried about some other, less tangible, problem. Perhaps it was a lack of money, I thought. Maybe there was another child on the way. Either one, or neither one, was a possibility. She was just one of those people who beg to be explored, layer by layer.

But the thing that thrilled me most, as an artist, was the contrast between her perpetual worry and world-weariness on the one hand and the look of wide-eyed naive wonder on her children's faces. The contrast was striking, even profound.

I wanted very much to paint them, and so I followed them.

I soon found out what *it* was. A parade was marching down Commerce Street, one of the major downtown thoroughfares just a few blocks from the Square.

The boys chattered happily. Their mother fretted over them, trying her best to keep her brood clutched around the hem of her skirt. They took up a spot on a street corner and the boys climbed up on a green metal lamp post so they could have a better look.

From where I sat on a bus stop bench across the street I had a perfect view of them, and I began to draw.

Soon the parade arrived; pretty girls in prom dresses waving to the crowd from the rumbleseats of old-timey cars; marching bands; Shriners in go-carts; black men on horseback dressed up as Buffalo Soldiers. The boys were delighted, and I drew at a frantic pace, trying to put it all down on paper.

The crowd pressed closer to the street, their mouths open and a gasp on their lips as a man on a ten foot high unicycle rode by, juggling flaming torches.

Somebody pressed up against me, and his thigh bumped my elbow, sending my pencil scratching across the page where I'd nearly finished drawing the mother's face.

"Hey," I said. "Watch it, buddy."

But when the man looked down at me, my mouth went dry and I couldn't breathe.

He had no face, no features whatsoever.

I gasped for air and stumbled to my feet. The man seemed unaffected by my fear, oblivious to it, and as my mouth worked desperately to say something he turned away and melted back into the crowd.

Only then did I notice the other people in the crowd, for all of them were strangely out of focus. The people nearest me had dark pits for eyes and an unformed hump for a nose and a red slash for a mouth, but beyond them, in the ranks of spectators in the background, the faces became less and less distinct, the features disappearing entirely. It was like looking at a photograph of a large crowd, a seething mass of humanity that became blurrier as the perspective lengthened. To my horror, I realized I was surrounded by the indistinguishable props that made up that photograph.

Panic overwhelmed me.

I think I screamed.

I dropped my sketchbook on the sidewalk and stumbled out into the street and right into the middle of the trumpet section of a marching band.

Their music became a jumble of ruined notes, and cries of protest mixed with jeers of laughter rose up from the crowd. I couldn't process any of that, though. I was too frightened, too rattled, to register the confusion I was creating.

Suddenly a pair of hands grasped me roughly by my collar and spun me around. I found myself facing a barrel-chested policeman, whose great bulk was easy enough to see, but whose face was a blurred shifting of half-discernable features.

"What the hell's your problem?" he demanded.

His voice sounded like a tape cassette being eaten by a tape player.

I fumbled for words, but couldn't say them.

"Are you drunk?" he croaked.

"No," I managed. I couldn't meet his melting eyes. His mouth drifted from one side of his chin to the other.

He picked me up and dragged me through the crowd, which spread open for us like a zipper.

The next thing I knew, I was being thrown into a garbage heap.

"Get lost," the garble-voiced policeman said. "I see you again, I'll take your ass to jail."

I dragged my aching body into an alley and climbed to my feet. Blinded by confusion and half mad with fear, I ran back to the Square and headed up the stairs for the safety of my apartment.

-SOH-

And I heard the scratching again. It grew louder the closer I got to third floor landing. It seemed to come from Suffles' apartment and from inside my head at the same time. I don't really know how to describe it, except to say that it was weird, and wrong, and so persistent and emotionally painful that it almost made me cry.

Wesley Suffles came out of his apartment as I was climbing the last few stairs to the third floor landing.

"Hello," he said happily. He was fully clothed, and he appeared to be sober.

"Hello," I answered, trying to sound cool, but still with desperation in my voice, and probably in my eyes. Standing there, I was aware of the garbage smell that still lingered on my clothes.

Perhaps he thought I was afraid of him, because his voice was oddly gentle, almost parental.

"Listen," he said, "I'm sorry about the other night. I realize now that I must have seemed out of my head."

"Perfectly all right," I said, fumbling through my pockets for my keys.

All I wanted to do was get inside and forget about the weirdness I'd seen at the parade, but he wouldn't let me go that easily.

He followed me to my door and said, "It's just that it caught me by surprise, you know? Seeing you here?"

Something about the way he said it unsettled me. Was I supposed to know him or something?

"I'm afraid I don't know what you're talking about," I said.

"Well, surely you can imagine my surprise. It's not the kind of thing that happens every day, you know. I mean, wouldn't it rattle you if the subject of one of your paintings suddenly stepped off the canvas and struck up a conversation with you?"

The man must sniff glue, I thought.

"Mr. Suffles," I said, "what in the world are you talking about?"

"You really don't know?" he said, his expression incredulous. He tried to smile.

"Know what?"

"Who *you* are, man! Who *I* am!"

"I think," I said, "that we ought to say good day."

I threw the bolt with my key.

"Please don't go," he said. "This must scare you horribly. I'm sorry. I didn't intend to scare you."

"What is it you think scares me, Mr. Suffles?"

"Why, meeting me, of course. The man who created you. The man who wrote you into being."

I blinked. In my mind, I saw Suffles' status drop

from alarmingly insane to pitiable and foolish.

"I'm turning in for a nap," I said.

"I know you," Suffles said urgently, desperate that I believe him. "I know you better than any one. Better even than you know yourself."

It sounded like a challenge.

"You do, eh? What do you think you know, Mr. Suffles?"

"Okay," he said, smiling, eyes darting back and forth, like he was trying to find his place in a script only he could read. "Okay. Remember that skinny little Hispanic girl in your office back in St. Louis?" He winked at me obscenely. "The one with the killer ass? You remember her, don't you? She wore that tight little yellow skirt her first day. Her little black thong was showing over the top of her skirt every time she sat down. After you saw that you went back to your office and spent the rest of the day with your hand in your pocket, rubbing your cock. Remember that?

"And remember that day you came home and your wife told you she was pregnant with your oldest boy? How about that one, eh? You ran out of the house and went to that little bar with the palm trees out front. The front looked like a wrecked boat. Remember that? You got drunk and tried to think of a way to tell her to get an abortion because you didn't think you could handle it and you hated yourself because of how weak you thought you were. Remember staying out all night? Remember waking up in your car the next morning? The jerk in the car behind you blowin' his horn 'cause the light had changed and you didn't know it? And remember how—"

"Stop it!" I yelled. The horror I had felt at the parade was flooding back into me, harder than ever. "Stop it. You don't know me."

"William, think about it," he said. "Don't I know you? Aren't you asking yourself how I know what I know right now?"

"You're insane," I said, though at that moment I felt much less sure of my own grip on reality than of his. What he was saying...it was impossible. But it was all true. Every word of it. All those things had really happened.

"You are the finest character I've ever written," he said. "I've written thousands of them, William. I filled Cattleman's Square with their stories, their lives. But of all the characters, *you* William, *you* are my favorite."

"You mean...all of this?" I said, and waved my hand vaguely in the air. "All of this is in your head?"

I felt seasick.

"That's right," he said, nodding gravely. "You understand."

"No," I said.

He was completely unperturbed by my denial.

"I did something for you I've never done before or since, William. I gave you free will. I gave you the greatest gift I had to give."

"Stop it," I said.

"Don't you see, William?" he said. He took a few steps towards me, his hand stretched out before him lovingly, like a father to a son. "That's why I was surprised to see you here. I wrote a story for you, what I thought would be your last. But you were more than that. You demanded to be more. You jumped right off the page."

I shook my head desperately, denial pulsing in me like a wild heartbeat.

"You're more than I gave you credit for," Suffles said. "It restored me, waking up to that realization.

24

And I'm writing more stories for you now too." He was breathless, excited. "I've heard you've taken up painting. That makes me happy. I've written success into your story now. Just you wait. Good things are gonna start happening for you."

I was shaking with rage, with denial, with fear. I tried to speak but couldn't. My mouth was working like I was chewing gum, and I still couldn't answer.

Suffles put out his hand again, inviting me to take it.

God help me, I actually came close to doing it.

But I didn't. Instead, I stared at his offered hand, then closed my eyes. Without saying another word I turned the doorknob to my apartment and went inside.

-SOH-

Late the next evening, I was sitting on the floor in the corner of my apartment, my hands over my ears, trying to shut out the noise of that pen scratching.

There was a knock at my door. It was a spindly, skinny, white-haired little old woman in her early seventies. She was dressed all in purple—purple slacks, purple short-waisted sport coat, a light purple silk blouse with frills down the front. Her low-heeled shoes were purple. She even had webs of purple veins showing through the skin on the backs of her hands.

She held my sketchbook under her arm.

"William Barton?" she asked uncertainly.

"Yes?"

She held the sketchbook out to me with both hands. "I believe this is yours," she said.

I looked at it, then took it from her. "Thanks."

She smiled, but didn't leave. We stared at each other.

"Um," she said.

"Yes?"

"This is rather awkward. I found that in the street. After the parade?"

"Oh, yes."

"I hope you don't take offense, Mr. Barton, but I looked through your work."

"Oh?"

"They're very good," she added abruptly.

"Oh. Thank you."

"I don't suppose," she said, wringing her hands

with obvious unease, "that you're a painter?"

I told her that I was.

"My name is Gloria Hearns," she said. "By any chance, have you ever heard of me?"

"I'm afraid not, Ms. Hearns," I said. "Sorry."

"Gloria, please," she said. She handed me her card.

Gloria Hearns
Blue Star Art Gallery
414 Pioneer Way
San Antonio, Texas

"Blue Star?" I asked.

"That's my gallery," she said. "It's the largest in South Texas."

"Really?"

"Oh, yes." She smiled gracefully. "In a way, it's lucky for both of us that I found your sketches."

"Oh? How's that?"

"Well," she said, "I think we can help each other out." She glanced around the landing with distaste. She was obviously not one who appreciated poverty. "May I come in?"

"Oh," I said, remembering my manners. They'd sort of slipped out of daily usage with me. "Sure. Come in."

I stepped aside and she came in, her face a mixture of horrified repugnance at the mess, which was considerable, and fascinated surprise at the few paintings she could see.

She went right for my self-portrait, the one of me in the shattered mirror.

"My God," she said. "I knew it. I knew I was doing the right thing by coming here."

She turned to me and said, "Mr. Barton, I just knew this was a good idea. How would you like to exhibit your paintings in my gallery? A small run at first, maybe ten paintings. But after that..." She spread her arms expressively.

I was speechless.

"I could even offer you an advance," she said. "Would three thousand be okay? That would only be an advance, of course. Any of the paintings I see here could easily fetch three or four times that."

I still had my hand on the door knob when she said that, and the door was still open. From across the landing I heard Suffles' door open, and I happened to glance that way as I was closing the door.

Our eyes met, Suffles and mine.

He smiled, nodding enthusiastically. He even gave me a ridiculous *thumbs up* gesture. Right on! That a boy!

I had been on the verge of joy, but seeing Suffles, and seeing him give me that sign, brought back the weirdness of our last conversation, and my expression soured.

"Mr. Barton?" Gloria Hearns said. She looked concerned, like she was afraid she'd offended me or something.

"Three thousand is a very good rate for a new artist," she said. "I assure you of that. With your talent, of course, and a show or two under your belt, you'll soon be able to demand much more. And you keep the money you make from the sale of your exhibits. Minus twelve percent for the gallery, of course."

"Of course," I said, and closed the door.

Funny, how you can think volumes in only a moment. As I stood there, suddenly aware that I was holding my sketchbook, I thought back on everything

Wesley Suffles had told me. I thought back on his ridiculous claim that he was my creator, my God, my Frankenstein, but rather than laugh, I had to fight an inward struggle to keep my knees from buckling.

Was it really possible? Surely not.

But yet, he'd never misspoken a single word. That time he told me that laundry list of things he knew about me, all of them were true, and there was absolutely no way that anyone outside my own head could have known them all.

And there was my own strange behavior, the day the Greyhound bus I'd taken from St. Louis had stopped in San Antonio for a two hour layover. My ticket had been for Mexico. My intention was to lose myself on some Iguana-crowded beach and slowly self-destruct like a character in a Tennessee Williams play. But when I saw San Antonio, when I smelled its air and heard its sounds, something about it pulled at my gut like I was circling a black hole. I stepped off the bus, and with my head a twisted wreck of conflicting fears, I walked until I landed in Cattlemen's Square. It was like coming home, and the feeling was so powerful, so undeniable, that I just stayed.

I also thought of the parade, and the melting faces in the crowd. They were unfinished somehow, not completely realized, and that's when it hit me. *All of Cattlemen's Square was a figment of Wesley Suffles' imagination.* When I looked out my window, what I saw was a picture of his mind. Everything there was his creation, and as such, had only the depth, the texture, the history, that he had written for it. Those faces in the crowd were incomplete, not because there was some defect on their part, but because they were what Suffles needed for his fiction, a crowd, and nothing more.

It all fit, and I couldn't deny it.

And there was that sound, the constant scratching of his pen on paper.

I thought of the refrain from Poe's masterpiece, "The Tell-Tale Heart." *It's the beating of his hideous heart. That's what it is, the beating of his hideous heart.*

"Mr. Barton?" Gloria Hearns said, her voice betraying an edge of fear. Could she see the hatred in my eyes, I wondered.

"Ms. Hearns," I said, and laughed out loud when she straightened herself up and tried to look like she hadn't just seen the devil in my eyes. "Ms. Hearns, who sent you here?"

Her mouth, her old woman lips, trembled. "What do you mean?"

"You know you're a pawn, don't you?"

She shook her head. "I'm sorry," she said indignantly. "I don't understand what you're talking about."

"How much background did he write for you, Ms. Hearns? I've always heard an author should know more about his characters than he puts on the page. How deep did he go with you?"

I started to advance on her, and she, in sudden terror, backed up against the wall.

"Where did you go to high school, Ms. Hearns?"

"What? Mr. Barton, what—"

"Who was the first boy you kissed? What was his name?"

"I—"

"You don't know, do you?"

"Mr. Barton, please."

I had her there, I knew it. Had her figured out.

One of my paintbrushes was on the table next to the door, a heavy gauge #6 with a thick wooden handle, and I picked it up like a knife.

"You know what really pisses me off?" I asked her.

She shook her head. Her whole body shook.

"Not so much that my history has been rendered meaningless. That's not what pisses me off. I mean, hell, I gave that up voluntarily. No, what really pisses me off is that my *future* has been taken from me too."

I smiled at her, wickedly.

"I mean, look at it from my perspective. How can I be truly successful if I don't earn it? You see what I mean?"

She shook her head again, violently now.

"No," I said. "Of course you don't. You don't need that understanding to function in the role he made for you. The problem is though, *I've* got that understanding. I've got it up to my freakin' ears. I know it's not my talent that brought you here. It was him. He wrote you into my life."

The poor thing looked like she was going to rattle herself to pieces.

"I don't blame you, Ms. Hearns. Don't think that. I know this isn't your fault. You didn't ask for this."

I walked towards her and she put up her hands like she actually had a snowball's chance of stopping me. It was sad in a way.

-SOH-

Several hours later, my apartment was dripping with her blood. The floor was covered, as were most of the walls. I even managed to get wet little chunky bits of her on the ceiling.

It was exhilarating, and when it was finally over, I fell back onto my butt and looked at my trembling hands.

Drunk with the joy that I was finally taking control of my circumstances, I threw open my door and walked out onto the landing like a man who has just been saved.

Wesley Suffles was coming up the stairs, a bag of groceries in his hands.

"William," he said. He had that patronizing paternal smile on his face. But then he saw the blood on my hands. "William?"

He dropped his groceries and ran up the stairs. "William?" He grabbed my hands and turned them over in his while I laughed out loud.

Our eyes met.

He looked past me, through the open door to my apartment, and saw a glimpse of the scene inside.

He nearly puked.

"Oh my God," he said, his hand cupped over his mouth. "William, what have you done?"

I laughed at him, and when he walked into my apartment, I laughed at his back.

He came back out to the landing and closed my door behind him. The effort he made to stay calm was impressive.

"William," he said, pulling me away from the stairs. "My God, why did you do it? She was going to help you. She was going to make you a star."

He took a moment to look over the railing, to make sure we weren't overheard, and then said, "Okay, I can fix this. I can get you out of this. Let's see, I'll need a gangster. No, wait—Ah! I've got it. Come on." He pulled me towards his apartment. "I'm going to write a story for you that'll get you out of this."

He opened his door and we went inside. The apartment was almost completely bare of furnishings. There was no dresser, no coffee table. His bed was an old, yellowed mattress in the corner with a moth-eaten blanket over it. The only other piece of furniture was a plain wooden desk and a plain wooden chair in the middle of the room.

Handwritten manuscripts were piled everywhere. In some places, you couldn't even see the wall. There were mountains upon mountains of manila folders stuffed with loose leaf notebook paper, and every single page was crammed with a tight, surprisingly neat handwriting that contained all the lives of Cattleman's Square.

I didn't consciously look for my stories—at least not at first. Only after a few minutes of digging through the papers, listening to the steady scratching of Suffles' black ballpoint pen on the pages at his desk, did I realize what I was looking for. Once I knew what I wanted though, my search became desperate.

Suffles' apartment had two north-facing windows, just like mine, and they were open. A cool breeze drifted into the apartment, carrying with it the sound of a crowd gathering in the Square and the sound of workmen hastily hammering something together.

But I ignored all that. I had a mission, a need to know the truth, and I dug for it until, at last, I found a pile of yellowed papers in a far corner, stacked waist-high from the floor.

My name was printed in bold letters on the top page, and it was with a hitch in my chest that I removed it.

My life was there, reduced to fiction. I read in horror as one by one the milestones of my life replayed on the page. Here was the time when I was eleven, when my older brother Russell drowned. Here was the first tit I ever cupped in my hand. It belonged to a fat, acne-scared girl who gave it to me during a game of spin the bottle. I found my first car; my first love; my first heartache; my sons; the death of my father; my mother's stroke and subsequent senility; my wife; my divorce; my every glaring, ugly fault.

I sat on the floor and covered my face with my hands. "Why did I have to be like this?" I said.

The pen scratching stopped. "What did you say?"

"Why?" I asked him. "Why did I have to be this way?"

"William—"

"You gave me bad knees and bad eyesight and an ugly temper. You made me ugly and petty and worthless. You're a mean, sadistic son of a bitch, you know that? You could have made me beautiful. You could have made me skinny. You could have made my sons respect me and my wife love me. But you didn't do any of those things. You made me as mean and petty and weak as you are. Why? What possible reason could you have for being so cruel?"

"William," he said, "stop it, please."

But I didn't want to stop it. I charged him, and when I put my hands on him, I began to flail with my fists until his nose was gushing blood and his lips were cracked open and pulpy, like smashed peaches.

He scrambled away from me in terror. His black ball point pen was on the desk and I took it up. I stabbed at him with it, and when he crossed his arms over his face in a futile attempt to block me, I nailed the pen through his hand.

He screamed, then moaned. It was a low, horrible sound so pregnant with pain it seemed to shake the walls. I stared at the wound, and at him, and when he turned and ran, I followed him.

I chased him down the stairs and into the

hardware store on the ground floor. He turned then, his face that of a scared animal, and I beat him again. I punched and kicked him until I was too tired to swing my fists anymore, and then I sat down near the front counter and watched him as he crawled down the aisle with the hammers and nails.

Renewed anger washed over me, and I got up and followed him, picking up a hammer as I closed on him. "You can rewrite me, can't you? You can start me over. Make me young?"

"No," he said.

"No you can't or no you won't?"

"No," he said. His hands were in the air, the pen still sticking through the right one.

I took a swing at him with the hammer and it sent him into a frenzied panic to get away. His arms spun like pinwheels, and he landed on spools of chain and barbed wire, fell to the ground, and got up again.

"Stop!" he screamed.

But I didn't. I ran at him again, and he ran for the Square.

I stopped in the doorway.

There, in the middle of the Square, was a large

crowd, and at the center of the crowd was a large wooden structure—a gallows.

Understanding hit me like a truck.

"Your story," I said to him. "I thought you said you were going to write me out of trouble. Is this what you meant? You were going to have me hanged."

"No," he said. "This isn't for you. It isn't."

You're lying. I can see it in every crease in your face.

There was no point in prolonging what had to be done. With everyone watching in horrified silence, I stalked after Wesley Suffles, cornered him near the base of the gallows, and bludgeoned him to death with the hammer.

There were perhaps three hundred witnesses to my crime, and not a single one raised a hand to stop me. Not even when I dropped the hammer on the ground next to Suffles' body. Not even when I pulled the ball point pen out of his hand. Not even when a black pall spread across the sky, blotting out the first delicate rays of the sunrise in the east and smothering the stars in the plum-colored sky.

Those idiots...they'll never know why the sun

won't ever rise again, even though they were witnesses to the event. I pitied them for their ignorance, and I pitied myself because I knew the truth.

What a horrible, horrible thing it is to be free.

-SOH-

So here I sit, writing the final lines in this nasty little tale, making my own nasty little scratching noises.

After I went back inside and closed the metal accordion grill across the entrance to the building, I had to struggle with my mind for direction. Every decision was like pulling my feet out of mud. But at last I decided on this...this...what? A confession? A history? What can I call this?

I suppose, really, that it doesn't matter. In a few moments I'll be dead, and this thing, this whatever it is, will be all that's left.

When I'm done with this, this thing that I've written with my creator's ball point pen, I'll stack the loose leaf pages that it's written on and stash them under the loose floorboard in the corner of my apartment. But you know that, don't you? If you're reading this, you obviously found the loose board.

To you, whoever you are, please—

Ah! They're through the accordion grill I pulled across the door to the hardware store. Only moments left now.

If you find this, please, know that I'm not insane. I'm not. I almost wrote: *You've got to believe me!* but I figure, what's the point? I'm past the point where that matters. At least from my perspective. Perhaps it will matter to others. It doesn't to me.

Not anymore.

I merely wanted to silence the endless scratching of pen on paper, the beating of his hideous heart. But it seems that in the process of doing that, I've silenced my own hideous heart.

THAT DAMNED BOX

Matt Staggs

I was walking to the gas station to start my shift when I saw the box sticking halfway out of the dirt at a construction site. Nobody was around on account of it being about a quarter till eleven at night, so I hopped over the low-slung barbwire fence and, with a quick look over my shoulder, pulled it out of the dirt and shoved it under my jacket.

It was about the size and shape of a big shoe box, and was made of some kind of stained black leather. Along the side were three small silver clasps. There was something about it that gleamed of wickedness. It might have been the strange crimson stain, or maybe the way the leather felt—prickly, like maybe there were still hairs on it here and there.

It had a satisfying heft to it. It felt important. I felt important, as a matter of fact. Imagine me—the two-time loser, hard-core junkie that I am—finding this thing. Hell, it could be anything. Gold doubloons, like in the pirate movie starring that eyeliner-wearing Hollywood poof. Maybe even the goddamn Ark of the Covenant, or some such shit. Maybe I was meant to have found it.

I would have to open this in private, for sure. Hiding the box underneath my jacket, I zipped up, and started walking. I liked the way the box clinked against the token I kept on a chain against my chest. I got the little silver coin at group: a reward for six months of court-mandated sobriety. I walked the rest of the way to the gas station and clocked in to begin my shift.

I usually didn't get too many customers on the late shift, just the occasional trucker passing through. Even then, they didn't often stick around long. Just time enough to grab a cup of coffee and fill up their tanks. Most of the time, I had the place to myself.

I waited till the girl that worked the evening shift left, and I slid behind the counter. I took the box out from under my jacket and put it beneath the register, where I could look at it and stroke it on occasion.

I rang up five gallons of unleaded and a pack of off-brand rubbers for an embarrassed teenage boy.

After he left, I looked around the store—once left and once right—and pulled the box out onto my lap. I let out a deep breath and reached for the tiny silver clasps. I worked each clasp, one at a time. Each let loose with a click that was enormous inside the tiny little store.

I gingerly lifted the lid, and took a deep breath. This could be it for me, my ticket out of here. I was prepared for near about anything to be in that box. Anything but what turned out to be in there.

You know those big white grubs you sometimes find when you're digging a hole in the ground? They're fucking nasty, slimy looking things; fat and pale with six little legs. Goddamn horror show material. Well, imagine one of those bastards, times about ten, and that's what I found in the box. At least, that's what it looked like to me. The thing was about ten inches long, probably about four or five inches around. It was squirming in the box, its mandibles pinching open and closed, and its legs squiggling. I don't know why the thing was alive; maybe it was buried recently.

I don't spook easy, and I saw a lot of fucked-up shit when I was in lock-up, but this here wasn't just any kind of fucked-up, this was like something that crawled out of the devil's asshole. I was revolted.

I slammed the box's lid down, and was about to walk around the counter with it to go chuck it in the dumpster outside, when I heard the doorbell ring.

Shit. Customer. I stepped back around the counter.

"What can I do for you?"

He was a skinny greaseball with a face full of acne and a peach-fuzz moustache. Had on a cheap leather jacket and white high-top tennis shoes. Looked like a child molester. I can spot a chomo from a mile away.

He nodded, plunked down a six-pack of Fuzzy Navel wine coolers, and a bag full of Chew Fruit candies. Didn't even look up at me. Kept his eyes on the counter. Fucking bottomfeeder.

That's when I first heard the singing, if you want to call it that. It was coming from the box which, like a jackass, I had left on the counter. The song was high pitched, and I suppose, kind of pleasant. I'm not much of a music fan on account of me being what they call tone-deaf.

Mister Molester heard the music though, and he heard it loud and clear.

"Uh, hey, uh, what's that? Some kind of music box? Jesus, it's beautiful."

I felt kind of jealous as I watched him reach for the box. Fuck if I know why. Just a minute ago, I wanted to throw the thing out.

"Hey, asshole, that's mine and—"

Too late.

He reached for the lid and had it open before I could finish my sentence. Instead of the look of disgust that I expected to see upon his greasy face, the customer looked at the squirming grub like it was the most beautiful thing in the world.

The disgusting thing wriggled, its six legs twitching in the air, as the man reached to touch it. I was pretty damn spooked at that point.

As soon as he got his hand on the thing the music stopped, a freakin' shower of blood shot out of the box. He tried to pull his hand away, but there was nothing he could do. Whatever that grub thing was, it was strong and it was hungry. Meanwhile, the hapless wine cooler-buying bastard was screaming his head off.

47

That Damned Box

I dove under the counter looking for the old machete I kept for scaring off would-be robbers and other assorted scum. Usually gas station owners leave their employees with a pistol or shotgun for these purposes, but not the prick that runs this place. He hires a lot of us ex-cons, and doesn't trust us enough to have a real weapon. I snuck the machete in and hid it under a stack of phone books beneath the counter. I can't afford a pistol of my own, and really, the machete seems to work better. Young punk kids aren't scared of being shot; the dumbasses think life is like the movies and they can take a hunk of lead and keep walking. Something about the big-ass rusty machete does the trick though—potential dismemberment scares even the toughest thug.

Anyway, I pulled the thing out from under the counter and swung at the box. Unfortunately—at least for my customer—the blade went wide and sunk into his arm, severing his hand just above the wrist. He pulled away, grasping his stump with his one good hand, howling in pain as the blood pumped out in great pulsing spurts.

The thing in the box greedily devoured its meal, humming contentedly. The customer fell flat on the ground, jerking like he was having some sort of fit. Maybe he was going into shock or something. As I raised the machete to take another swing, the filthy grub in the box spat out the man's finger bones. They clattered on the counter, next to the lotto ticket sign and the disposable lighters, and the box's lid swung shut with a loud click.

Suddenly, I wasn't so sure about what I should be doing with that thing. What would happen if I hit it with the machete and only pissed it off? What if it got out of the box when I threw it in the dumpster?

I dropped the blade on the floor behind the counter and walked over to the customer. He was still, now; no more jerking or twitching. I put my fingers on his neck to feel for a pulse. He was dead. I had a real problem now.

I couldn't exactly call the cops to help out. What would they say when I told them a big-ass worm killed the guy? Even if I showed them the grub it would be only my word—and as a junkie ex-con, my word wasn't worth shit. Two narcotics convictions, both felonies. They'd have my ass in lock-up before I even opened my mouth. We didn't have any video cameras in the store, either. I mean, we did, but they had been busted for a month. Cheap son of a bitch owner wouldn't fix them.

Well, fuck. I did what I could.

I grabbed the pervert's ankles and dragged his filthy ass across to the walk-in beer cooler. I pushed a few boxes of malt liquor around and shoved the corpse in far and deep. I had the rest of the night to clean up the mess and get the dead guy out of there. Dumping the body wouldn't be a problem. There are a few spots that I know from the bad old days, before I went down.

I stepped out of the beer cooler and got to work on all of the blood. There was plenty of it, too. Good thing about where I work, we've got a little bit of everything. Scoring a disposable mop and some bleach wasn't difficult.

I was just about halfway through cleaning up the mess, when I heard the doorbell ring. I pushed the mop and bucket behind the counter, and pulled a rack of corn chips over what was left of the blood.

In walked two little girls, trying their damndest to be women. Both of them had to be about 18 or so, dressed in tight skirts, and all dolled up in tons of makeup. I made my way over to the counter.

One of them, a short little brunette wearing a retainer, flashed me a smile.

"Excuse me, but we had a friend come in here a little while ago. Have you seen him? He's a little guy with a moustache. He was supposed to be getting something for us."

I knew the score. They were looking for the pervert in the freezer. They must have slipped him a few bucks to buy the wine coolers; they were too young to get on their own. Probably thought he gave them the slip. I could work with that.

"Yeah, little complexion problem? Dark hair? He was in here, but he left a few minutes ago."

She looked like she was going to buy it for a minute, but then her blonde friend, who looked like that rich heiress whore that's always on the television, joined us at the counter with questions of her own.

"Oh yeah? Well why didn't we see him? We've been waiting around the corner next to his van. If he left, why would he go on foot?"

"Listen, I don't know nothing about it. I saw him leave—"

Blondie cut me short.

"Haley, he might still be in the cooler. I'm going to go back there and look."

Shit. This was getting out of hand quick.

"Hey, uh, miss. Listen, I've got a maintenance problem back there, and you can't go in."

There was nothing doing. She was going in there no matter what I said, so I had to try to stop her. I stepped out from behind the counter and reached out to grab her arm. Just as I put my hand on her, I got distracted by that weird singsong noise coming from the box behind me. Apparently the brunette at the counter was too. I had left the thing in the box there when I was trying to get the store cleaned up. My bad.

When I turned to say something to the brunette, the blond slipped out of my grasp.

"Get away from me, you perv!" She stomped into the walk-in cooler.

The brunette stuck her hand inside the box, just like her buddy had. From behind, it looked like she had shoved her fist into a blender. The thing was literally eating her alive, inch by inch.

I ran over and tried to pull her away from the box, but all I ended up doing was pulling us both down on the ground, her on top of me with the grub still attached to the nub of her arm. The thing had gotten bigger somehow, and its hard little pincer mouth was going to town on her wrist. She was struggling and swinging her arm left and right with the thing on the end of it. I did my best to roll her over and pin her to the ground, hoping that I could pull the creature off of her. By that time, she had stopped struggling.

Flipping her over and pinning her to the ground was easier said than done; the fight must have gotten her adrenaline pumping and she was as strong as hell. I managed to get an elbow into her back, and her mangled arm pinned behind her shoulder blade, just in time to hear a scream from the freezer. Apparently, Blondie found the popsicle-pervert beneath the malt liquor.

I looked up from the bloody mess beneath me in time to find myself eye-to-eye with Blondie.

That Damned Box

"Ah, fuck. It's not what it looks like. Get over here and help me!"

She started screaming, and ran right back into the freezer. I could see her reaching for her rhinestone-encrusted cell phone through the frosted glass in the door. I got up and made a run for the freezer door, slipping in the fresh blood coating the tile floor. My feet went out from under me, and I slid the rest of the way to the door on my stomach. I got up and pushed my way inside.

She was cowering behind a stack of Mountain Stream 12-packs, trembling in the cold. She was trying her best to dial the tiny bejeweled buttons on her cell phone, but her frigid fingers weren't up to the task. I knocked the phone out of her hands and smacked her right upside her head. I never said I was a good guy, okay?

She went out like a light, and I pulled her by her hair over to where the dead guy was. I yanked the plastic rings off of a nearby six pack, bound Blondie's hands behind her back, and stepped out of the freezer to deal with the mess on the floor.

The hapless brunette was missing most of her arm now, and the grub was grinding away on her making some sort of weird-ass purr, like some kind of cat. I stepped around it, and her, and went for the machete behind the counter. Damn the consequences, I thought, this had to end.

"It's alright pal, just keep enjoying your meal," I muttered as I reached my hand behind the counter and wrapped my fingers around the machete's handle. The thing gnawed and gnawed, happy as a pig in shit.

I swung the machete over my head and straight down in an attempt to cut the thing in two. It was too quick for me and caught me by surprise. The thing lifted up on its little stubby legs and scuttled away with a high-pitched shriek. My machete hit the tile, and I'll be damned if the thing didn't snap at the handle. I looked up in time to see the grub disappear beneath a rack of candy bars. Bastard!

I ran one aisle over and grabbed a can of hairspray and a lighter. I got down on my hands and knees, where I saw the thing disappear, and I shot a gout of flame underneath the rack. I could see it under there, near the back. It was hiding, clacking its little jaws at me, and singing that strange little song. It didn't have any effect on me. I reached my hands in a little closer to the creature and prepared to fry its creepy ass. I would have gotten it too, except that some melting candy from the shelf above me dripped onto my hands. I hissed in pain and dropped the hairspray. That's when the creature made its move.

Rather than gnawing off one of my fingers, it pivoted around, and sunk an inch-long stinger into my hand. It hurt like a bastard, but after that, I was in junkie heaven. I got a huge rush, like the thing had pumped me full of the heaviest shit I'd ever seen. I slowly crawled away from the creature's hiding place and nodded out in the aisle.

I woke up a few minutes later and found the grub lying in my lap. It had retracted its stinger deep into its body, and was sort of purring; flexing its little legs as it rested.

I had a moment of revulsion, and then that familiar hunger was upon me. I was hooked. I didn't know what kind of poison this thing was dealing, but I knew I wanted more of it. I tried to coax the stinger out of its tail-end, but it wasn't working. The thing mewled piteously and clacked its little mouth parts together. I sensed that it needed to eat. Well, I needed to get high, so perhaps we could work something out.

I got up and took the creature into the beer cooler, where I had left Blondie. By this time, she was awake, and was struggling against her make-shift bonds. Her little skirt must have worked its way loose and down her thighs, because I caught an eyeful of her snatch. My cock didn't even stir—all I cared about was my next fix. She saw the grub in my hands, and she started to scream and plead with me. I was beyond all that now and just placed the creature on her abdomen. It started to dig in almost immediately, and soon she stopped shouting and just sort of laid there. After a while, it crawled off of her and curled up on the floor. I bent down, scooped the thing up, and walked out of the cooler.

Within a minute or two of walking out of the freezer, it revealed its stinger and gave me another dose of the good stuff. I hardly remember what I did next. If I think real hard, I can sort of recall grabbing the thing's box and stuffing it back into it. The next thing I remember is dousing the whole store down with lighter fluid and day-old newspapers, before tossing a match behind me and locking the door.

After that, I sort of blacked out.

When I came to again, I was sitting in the driver's seat of a van—I'm guessing the pervert's wheels—at some rest stop in the middle of nowhere. I wasn't alone, though. I had the grub, and as long as I could keep it well-fed, the fix it gave me would never end. I patted the box affectionately, turned the key in the ignition, and got moving. The thing in the box began to sing its little tune as we pulled onto the highway.

Somebody was hungry.

Tyranny of the Beat
John Edward Lawson

"We need to speak with the pathos on duty."
Oceana and Voshawn have been summoned from
their paperwork. Like most detectives, they prefer
paperwork to actually leaving the police station.

"We have *pathologists* on duty, yes," the
receptionist states, rankled by their abbreviation of
the doctor's title. "You here about the dead girl?"

"What do you think?"

"Right." The woman pushes a button and goes
back to reading a magazine.

Voshawn would describe himself as a detective
from the "old school" who is willing to get the job
done at any cost. Over the years he's gone from
having rugged good looks to just being rugged. He
keeps his dark hair as short as possible to deny
opponents something to hold onto during fights.

Oceana would describe herself as hard-edged,

perhaps even more so than her partner. While she is newer to the police force she makes up for it with her fervor. She leaves her blonde hair long so others will fall prey to stereotypes and think her a bimbo letting their guard down, despite the fact "blonde jokes" drive her into a rage.

Prefabricated mood music drifts in, a stale affront to their sensibilities. Although designed to soothe these songs only serve to further agitate the duo.

Eventually a tiny, mental-looking man waddles out, older, squinting behind his grease-smeared glasses. He looks the detectives over, shakes his head. "Come on," he says, gesturing.

The pair follows him to the back, listening to him spew details of the case. The young woman in question made her way down a heavily trafficked road assaulting at least sixteen people before succumbing to one that didn't want to be her victim. No name, no information to go on. Oceana looks to her partner, and they are both thinking: *just like all the others recently.* The group makes their way through the hibernation ward until reaching the patient's room. She lays stretched out before them like a corpse, nude, with a dozen wires and tubes extending from her skin to various machines.

"We're working to achieve metabolic quiescence," he tells them. This is old news, but he continues to explain the process for no reason other than to hear his own voice. "Hydrogen sulfide, normally toxic in high doses, is introduced to the patient's system at 80 parts per million, reducing the metabolic rate to the point that oxygen almost isn't necessary. With all major organ systems at a standstill the patient breathes through their skin only, and we can take the opportunity to go about lengthy measures to repair any damage."

The detectives, they aren't even paying attention to him by this point, instead focusing on the body itself. "Notice all the scarring? Especially there and there." Oceana points out the hands and knees. "Check out the bruising, too."

"I saw. Even worse than the abused wives we see, or the slaves from South America."

"Yes," the doctor interjects. "Obviously the result of prolonged physical injury, of an escalating nature judging from the severity and depth of the more recent physical traumas."

They spend a moment studying the body in

silence, taking notes.

"Her pubis appears well-worn."

The three glare at each other for a tense moment.

Oceana sighs, rolls her eyes. "What's the deal here, anyway? We're homicide."

"Yes. We have initiated the hibernation procedure, but our analysis indicates she may potentially be in a permanent vegetative state."

"Brain dead," Voshawn states, hawking up a wad of phlegm to spit on the floor.

The doctor stares at the detective's phlegm quivering on the bloody tile. "As I understand the new laws, actions leading to brain death are now capitol offenses."

Oceana replies, "But you're not positive she's in a vegetative state."

Noticing her smirk the doctor asks, "Do you doubt the validity of our procedures?"

"It's not that. On the way in I noticed all the women in the hibernation unit are so attractive. I'm wondering if you let the ugly ones die, and how many of the rest wake up in six months with a surprise pregnancy."

The doctor's jaw goes slack. "What are you trying

to insinuate?!"

Voshawn steps up, face to face with the old man. *"I don't like doctors."*

"I am a man of science!"

"Knowledge corrupts, doc."

Oceana nudges her partner. "Don't waste your breath telling him what he already knows."

The doctor straightens up, regains his composure. "We're not so different, doctors and detectives. We both rely on the scientific method to solve cases we're presented with."

"Fuck the scientific method," Voshawn grumbles as he shoves the doctor against a tiled wall.

Before the man can respond Oceana grips his face, her polished fingernails digging deep into his cheeks. "Don't try to lump us in with your lot, you pervo screwhead."

Voshawn adds a punch to the man's belly for good measure. "We're not interested in waiting a month for the report, doc. Have it to us tomorrow or we'll come down here and get it ourselves. Understand me?"

The doctor grovels at their feet, his response rendered incomprehensible by strangled sobs.

"My partner asked you a question!" Oceana kicks the man. "Answer him!"

The man's feeble nod is satisfactory. The detectives exit the morgue, knocking several folders and specimens to the floor on their way out.

-SOH-

Oceana sits at her desk, listening to the latest casualty estimates from the war. The furniture of her office is piled high with reports, crime scene photos, computer disks, witness testimony on DVD, gas masks and other state-issued survival gear. While dialing a phone number she listens as rusty rainwater trickles into the network of buckets scattered across the floor. Half of the piled papers and evidence have been rendered useless by mildew.

"Hey V. Got the coroner's report."

"Hey O," comes her partner's voice. Then, "Great."

"Did I wake you?"

"I was just in bed."

"You don't sound so good," she says, closing her office door against the noise of the central booking room. "What happened? Yesterday you were on cloud

64

nine."

"Let's just put it this way," he says, stopping to slurp down a drink. "Yesterday was the God mix, and today's just yesterday remixed by Satan."

She pauses. "Uh...right. You need to go back to sleep, saying weird shit like that."

"No, no, you got the report. Hit me with it."

She flips through the pages, drags a blood-red nail down to the line she's searching for. "Seems somebody did a number on our victim's neural system."

"Okay, what drug are we looking for? Something new?"

Irritated by coworkers interrupting the conversation, she puts him on hold. A minute later, when she returns, she says, "We need to change our thinking on this one."

"Yeah?"

"Some kind of implants all up and down her nerves and spine, in her brain and whatnot. The pathos call it 'biotech of the highest order.'"

"Sounds fruity. They must be jealous, or dreaming."

"It's not another one of their pervo fantasies. They

sent pics, and a few samples retrieved from her tissue. I took a look at it all, but to be honest it means nothing to me."

"Well, it's got to mean something to somebody. We just need to find that person."

Oceana contemplates how to go about doing so, then grunts. "V."

"Yeah?"

"There was a tattoo on her shoulder. Do you have the photos handy?"

"Got 'em right here."

"I thought you said you were in bed."

Ignoring the remark he says, "Looks like a barcode, a circular one."

"Right. Certain nightclubs use them to allow patrons in."

"Shoulder scan? What kind of clubs are we talking about here?"

"Hardcore ones."

"And how would you know?"

Oceana clears her throat. "I have one, from back when I was in school."

"Back when you were in school."

"Sure. Maybe I'll show it to you sometime."

"Spare me," he says. "Just get on with it. These clubs have names or what?"

"I'm putting together a list now. Should have it to you in five minutes."

"Look, I want to put this thing to rest. You take half, I'll take half. Fair?"

"Sure. My barcodes will get me in at a few places. Shouldn't be hard to get information."

"'Barcodes?' As in plural? You some kind of hardcore raver chick?"

She ignores him. "I'll be logged in all night long. If you hear anything, anything at all, just text me."

"Yeah, yeah. Can I go now?"

"Sure. Good luck."

"Mm-hmm."

She hangs up, thinks about the club scene. If it has grown any more outrageous than during the wild years of her youth she may be in trouble.

-SOH-

Young people in varying stages of pre-suicide gather, some twitching, others nervously licking their lips, waiting for the doors of a warehouse to open. A large sign over the entrance reads THE GREAT BATTLE. Pipes hiss, smokestacks from the surrounding factories pump poison into the air, and finally a doorman steps out to inspect everyone's credentials.

This is when Voshawn confronts a trio of henchmen whose skin is never caressed by the sun. A feminized one in leather, he seems to hold seniority over the other two. While showing them his badge Voshawn watches their dead eyes, decides they're no more than zombies.

"I'm here to follow up on complaints regarding a series of disappearances. Some of your regular customers don't come home again."

The fem-boy crosses his arms, sneers. "Complaints?"

"That's right."

And the zombies, they laugh, something suddenly animate behind their eyes—the recognition of a lie.

As the door starts to slam in his face the detective thrusts himself forward, using his body to keep it propped open. The trio's demeanor suggests they have killed before and are eager to do so again. Voshawn, his glare would freeze lava. "Okay, I want to see Elder so I can cave in his face in with my boots. Happy now?"

The zombies, they look at each other, at Voshawn, then at each other again. Their conspiratorial whispering is obscured by a torture-beat hammering away within the club. Finally they turn back to him. "We'll need your guns. No weapons allowed inside."

After leaving his four handguns at the coat check they lead him deeper inside. Random Sexy People line the periphery, bursting out of their scanty clothes with ample bosom and muscle, glistening under the mood lighting, sultry and mysterious in their way. The truth is so many gorgeous men and women can be found in the halls, in the streets, filling up the background, that their animal magnetism fails. They are props, are part of the stage design, and no real person ever had sex with part of a stage set. At least, nobody would ever admit to it if they did. The Random Sexy People need not describe themselves, as they are constructed from societal clichés of beauty, woven from the facile whims of today's fashions.

Here inside the club the beat punches at

Tyranny of the Beat

Voshawn's organs while a distorted voice screams about celebrating the enemy. The worn fabric of his suit slides against oiled flesh as he presses through the gyrating throng. Somebody's elbow jabs his neck and he contemplates going for his gun. When a breast slaps into his face he realizes this is, against his intuition, an unpleasant experience. Perhaps under different circumstances Voshawn would be able to relax and enjoy himself. Of course, he's not quite the young sexy person the rest of the crowd is.

The three doormen fight off advances from inebriated women and men, ignore whatever inane questions or complaints people yell over the music. They nod to a bartender before opening a door at the rear of the club. Thus far, Voshawn hasn't seen any suspicious types lurking about, just the three he's already made contact with. It crosses his mind that perhaps he should have let Oceana know about this, but he dismisses the thought; she admitted being a club-goer, so she's probably whacked out on drugs, if not taking bribes from every lowlife bar in town.

The zombies lead him down an unlit, shaky staircase. In the basement is a hallway, at the end of which a laboratory awaits. Actually, it looks more

70

like a sloppy mechanic's workshop.

A silver-haired man in heavily stained work clothes peers at the group as they enter. This is Elder, who would describe himself as a web-dancer, a web-tripper, one who swings through the primordial jungle of neurons and glial cells like some postmodern Tarzan. Even deeper still he break-dances and body pops among the very components of the neural cells: the basal dendrites, the axon, the synaptic terminals. Yes, terminal, all of his patients are, quite naturally. He himself is facing the business end of the Grim Reaper's scythe, old as he is.

He waves the zombies away. Once they leave, he asks, "How is it you came to know of us, detective?"

"Give me some credit, doctor. A detective is trained to pick up on the subtle vagaries of witness statements."

Elder observes the splatter of what looks like blood on Voshawn's pants leg, observes the rawness of his knuckles. "How very...proficient of you."

"Whatever. I hear you're the man to talk to about all this weird body modification that's going down."

"Oh?"

"Oh? Oh! Yes, 'oh!' Are you aware these body

mods of yours are killing people?"

After scrutinizing him it's clear just how drained Elder is. For all the detective knows he might drop dead right here and now. "The improvements I bestow upon those people...it would be ludicrous to assert my work has a negative effect on the physiologic process."

"So you admit it! You are the one." Not waiting for a reply, Voshawn steps forward, saying, "Let's get you to someplace a bit more suitable for discussion."

"Such as the police station?"

"You're a bright man, doc."

Elder turns to his equipment, begins to lay out his tools as if preparing for surgery. "You know, it only takes a few thousandths of a second."

"Um...excuse me?"

"For a signal to travel to your toes from your brain."

"Oh, right."

"It's because of the jumpers," the doctor continues, polishing his tools. "You've got Schwann cells at the ends of each neuron, which you can think of as service stations. The signal reaches the Schwann cell and has to jump across a chasm called the node of Ranvier."

The detective clears his throat. "In all honesty, this isn't school and I'm not being graded, doctor."

The old man raises his eyebrows. "You're not?"

Voshawn becomes aware of two men standing behind him. Two large men.

Elder coughs up bloody phlegm, examines it. "The outside of a neuron's plasma membrane contains a positive charge, while the inside maintains a negative charge. Any thoughts about this, you fascist bullyboy?"

"Yes," Voshawn answers while evaluating the doctor's thugs. "I'd like to rip your eyes out with pliers."

"Good, very good." Elder chuckles. "You have a fair grasp on the situation; traveling through the network that is society we maintain a decorous exterior—our positive side—all while harboring the darkest thoughts and desires within—our negative side. I merely reverse an individual's charge."

"The only charges you'll be seeing are the ones they'll throw at you in court." Voshawn gropes the space his gun should occupy. "You're really a bunch of hellmongers, aren't you?" When he jumps at Elder the two large men grab him, slam his smaller frame to the floor, bear down on him with all their weight.

"I suspect, dear boy, that you're more like a suppressor T cell, but we'll turn you into a jumper in no time."

-SOH-

Oceana is stirring her drink, glaring at the other patrons from the corner of her eye. It's not clear why her partner wanted to meet her in a place like this. When asked about his absence he simply called it time spent undercover. "I'm ready to blow this whole thing wide open," he had told her. What the "thing" in question was he didn't mention.

She still fits into her club clothes from the old days, even if they are a bit dated. Listening to the random noises pumped through the speakers she can't recall what was so attractive about clubbing to begin with.

"Hey O." Voshawn lurches out of the darkness, leaning in close, too close. His breath is moist with something unwholesome.

"You know how many pretty boys and girls have

gone into hibernation since you pulled your disappearing act?"

Ignoring her he scans the crowd, spits on the floor. "Not nearly enough..."

"What?" Surely she didn't hear that correctly.

"I've always liked all the action I saw on the force. So have you, O."

She finishes her drink. "I never said I didn't."

"You ever think we never reached our action potential?"

Oceana sizes up her partner. At first the strange leather clothes and spiked metal boots didn't bother her; she figured he was doing his utmost to blend with the crowd. Now, though, combined with his constant twitching and irrational conversation, she has to wonder. "V, what about the case—"

"An action potential works like this: the exterior of the membrane of a nerve cell is more positive than the inside, until sodium ions flood in changing the polarity. It's only once the membrane takes on a negative charge that things start happening."

"Things need to be negative to provoke changes?"

"Yes." He seems a bit too excited by the prospect.

"So what you're saying is all this random

violence, all these people behaving like animals, is really the basis of some nerdy revolution?"

"Revolution. Absolutely." His fist collides with her lips, her chin.

When she reels from his punch the anger in her eyes comes alive. She strikes a blow in return, and he makes no effort to defend himself. "What the hell, huh?"

He grins distractedly. "That wasn't bad, but maybe an EQ adjustment is in order..."

"EQ? Yeah, your EQ's all messed up." She turns to leave. That's when he hits her from behind, much harder this time.

-SOH-

Oceana and Voshawn have been reborn. Their hearing is acutely attuned to the sensations running the length of their nervous systems, the pain in particular. Such beautiful sounds were never meant for human ears.

They stand at the cusp of The Great Battle, a mosh pit filled with raving lunatics the detectives sought to capture in their previous life. The music here is beyond anything they have ever experienced. It is not the sound of instruments made by humans. The otherworldly tones are those of humans *made into* instruments. According to Elder, different points of the nerves correspond with different notes, like strings stretched over the neck of a guitar—a guitar neck in a guillotine, perhaps. The building's music system is modified to pick up and transmit a steady feed from Elder's handiwork, everyone's bodies loaded with artificial receptors and black market bio enhancements identical to those showing up in the hospitals, in the morgues. All members of this congregation sizzle with sensation in the throes of the Great Battle, slamming into each other, into walls, into tables, each impact adding to the kinetic artistry. The music blasting through the speakers is just the remixology of the patrons' pain.

The Great Battle holds no interest for Voshawn and Oceana. They leave that scene behind and hit the streets, injected into society's arteries once more.

-SOH-

It begins rather simply. The desire for sustenance

is replaced with an uncontrollable urge to inflict injuries on themselves. The crowded streets are not so different from the dank man-made caverns that host dance nights and performances. Out in the open space between buildings the sounds of random conversations and engines revving and wheels screeching mingle as abstract sound compositions, avant-noise, with plenty of flashing lights and cars bouncing to the rhythm. Some of the people are oblivious, others bear the mark. The bruises. The scars that serve as badges to gain entry into the city's most hardcore clubs.

Oceana intentionally steps into the path of a bicycle messenger. The collision sends them both sprawling to the pavement, bloodied. As the messenger curses, Voshawn looks on dispassionately carving lines in his forearm with a house key. Oceana leans over the angry messenger and kisses him, her mouth slimed with black blood—blackened with surging nanotech. Moments later the man calms down, the savage beast within settled by the opening strains of a requiem only he can hear. The adjustments being made to his nervous system translate his cuts into chords, broken bones into arias. Within a minute he is leaning on his twisted bicycle for support as he limps away.

The former detectives don't linger. Instead, they find the closest lounge. It turns out to be a jazz bar. Two minutes later they have been expelled, but two minutes is all they need.

Knowing that he wasn't long for this world Elder created his Sistine Chapel in these two police officers, these two pillars of society's structure. The biotech has spilled over into their bloodstreams not by fault, but by design. It is self-replicating, unlike the laborious handmade work Elder specializes in. The promise of harmonic ecstasy lures them into colliding with others, just as with Elder's older implants, but more than that these impacts are necessary for the biotech to spread. To infect. The need for an audio engineer like Elder has been eliminated all together.

In bar after bar, nightclub after nightclub, Oceana gazes across the havoc to her partner, drooling black blood and loving it. Lights flash while attractive people shake and thrash. Things speed up and slow down at random. She and Voshawn are starting to look badly damaged, but it's nothing a quick shower and cosmetics can't fix. Elder reinforced their bone structures, replacing cartilage with space-age polymers, ball-and-socket joints with stainless steel. True, the majority of their stitches have ripped loose but that only serves to add new instrumentation to their agonized orchestra.

Word spreads quickly among the security community, and police are told to be on the lookout for a pair of nutters. Soon, though, it makes no difference. The bicycle messenger has infected four others, who have infected seventeen others, who have infected sixty-three others. Violence escalates far beyond The Great Battle, spilling over into the streets, the slums, the business districts, a virus moving at the speed of sound—which, in this case, is about 130 beat(ing)s per minute. This is no St. Vitus dance; Death plays choreographer here.

Voshawn and Oceana slump to the ground, their dance curtailed by blood loss. The jagged reminders of Elder's subversive attentions leak black sludge as the couple convulses to a tune heard by their ears only, a song that fades with every heartbeat...

Guerilla forces have installed speakers under bridge supports, inside sewer drains, on rooftops.

They are equipped to pick up Elder's handiwork, and the alien sounds are amplified a thousand fold, terrorizing those who are not yet aware of the street violence. The ensuing confusion causes everything to grind to a halt. Most speakers emit solos to begin with, but as the impacts escalate solos become duets, become quartets, become symphonies of suffering. The city's vital signs become erratic, trying and failing to stave off an inevitable flat line.

Queen of Samhain
Louise Bohmer

"Lord, woman," Anna wiped Claire's feverish brow with a damp cloth, "how this obsession has aged you. I barely recognize you."

A weak smile crossed the withered face of her twin. "I could have fought this wasting of my body, had the Guild not stripped me of my charms." She ran a waxy hand down Anna's sculpted cheek, as a violent cough seized her and pulled Claire away from the straw mattress.

Leaning forward on the hard, rail-back chair, Anna rubbed between the ailing witch's shoulder blades. "It is not your body, but your soul that is languishing." She brushed a lock of ginger-grey hair from her sibling's sweat soaked neck. "I told you not to return to the woods after nightfall. Our kind is forbidden from joining in the revelries of the forest people. We are taught that from birth."

Lying back against her burlap pillow, Claire nodded and closed her glazed, green eyes. "I have betrayed the Oath of the Wise Women. I am a disgrace to the Guild."

Anna stroked the side of her sister's head and listened to her breathing deepen. "There is talk of sending you into exile."

"I know." Claire turned her head toward the small window carved into the thick wall of the two-room cabin. "I will not live to see exile. That is why I need your help."

The gnarled fingers of her feeble twin encircled Anna's wrist with a desperate strength. "I am too weakened to complete the task myself."

Rising from her chair, Anna sat beside her fragile sister on the tiny, driftwood cot. "What is it you would ask of me?"

Their eyes met, and the hunger, the madness, in Claire's sagebrush irises made her shiver. "I have trespassed in the sacred oak grove, sister." She bowed her head. "I have captured his queen."

Straightening her brown, muslin skirt, Anna folded her hands in her lap. "This is not your only secret. I know you have been to the exiles' camp, beyond the boundary of our hidden valley."

The weakened sorceress fidgeted with the dark, woolen blanket tucked across her breasts. "I know the Guild will never see my motives as valid, but you can understand my reasons can't you? I must have him." Her gaze lifted from her lap, and tears dampened her ashen cheeks. "Once you've laid with him …" She squashed her crumpled face into her palm and sobbed inside the protection of her hand. "His charm like a sickness."

Standing, Anna walked to the scant pane of glass, and watched the afternoon sun filter through the furry limbs of nearby pines. "The Oak King is best forgotten, sister. You would be wise to set his consort free and let her return to the underworld, before the rising of Samhain eve."

"But I can be his queen forever, if you will help me perform the Rite of Transformation."

Anna turned to face the foolish witch, with lips pulled tight in a thin, angry slit. "That is considered a black act by the Guild. If we are caught, it could mean execution, never mind exile."

Claire's eyes darted away, but not before Anna caught the spark of lunatic hope smoldering within.

Crossing the short distance to her sister, Anna stood over the bed, folding her arms tightly across the starched bib of her apron. "How did you manage to catch the Queen of the Forest? Was this another trick the exiles' taught you?"

"She ascends three days before the waking of the dead at Samhain. To rouse the King from his autumn slumber in the sacred grove. To take him below to prepare for the rising of the departed. I waited for her, at the entrance of the clustered oaks …"

"Where is she now?"

Claire shimmied up the rough headboard, clutching the meager blankets tight to her skeletal frame. "In the storage shed out back. I have shackled her in iron." Her large eyes dropped from Anna's; her cracked bottom lip trembled. "The metal will not injure her. It only binds her to a physical form."

Shaking her head, Anna sat, and wrapped her long fingers around the waning wise woman's shoulders. She stared deep into Claire's eyes, searching for a scrap of the sage, reserved woman that once dwelled within. "The exiles have taught you well indeed."

"Tell me then," she pulled back from her lost sibling, "how did you not wake the King when you took his lady?"

Claire looked away. "I was quiet and quick."

Dread built a tight cocoon around Anna's heart. She and Claire had never harbored secrets from one another. "You cloak your mind, so I cannot see your deeds, your heart."

Scowling, Anna rose from the bed and rubbed her tingling arms as she paced. Claire swung her legs over the edge of the straw mattress, and caught her about the waist as she passed.

"You still haven't answered me. Time grows short. I must have the Queen's blood before the full moon blooms this Samhain eve."

Anna pushed her away gently. Her hands fluttered to the nape of her neck, tucking wisps of coppery hair back into her loose bun. "What choice do I have?" Defeated, she dropped her head. "Without the transformation, you will perish. Tell me what I must do."

A crafty smile split the face of her dying twin. "I have the tools for the sacrifice underneath the bed. Would you bend and retrieve them for me, sister?"

Anna dipped to her knees, keeping her gaze fixed on the crazed Wise Woman. She tucked her arms beneath the meager cot. Her left hand fell upon something cold and metallic. The fingers of her right hand brushed against a rough, wooden surface. She gripped the hidden items and dragged them out. Her palm slipped down the onyx-handled dagger, pledged to Claire on their mother's deathbed. Beside it, sat a freshly carved birch bowl. Anna removed the silver-and-ebony dirk from its sheath and inspected the fine, steel edge.

"The blade that ends her life must be sacred to me." With a sheepish, yet wild-eyed look, Claire leaned over the bed and scooped up the plain basin in her trembling palms.

"Stab her in the heart. It is the seat of a wood spirit's essence. Bring the life fluid to me in this."

Anna clipped the scabbard to a small, silver belt beneath her apron, and took the vessel Claire held out to her. "And what becomes of me, dear sister, after your transformation is complete?" She clutched the bowl tight against her chest.

Claire fiddled with the ragged neckline of her nightgown. Her gaze darted toward the worn floorboards. "I will see you safely out of the valley. I will not leave you for the wrath of the Guild."

Hands flexing against the rounded sides of the basin, Anna let out a bitter rush of breath. "Your mortal spirit will die, Claire, as you take on the Wood Woman's form. You'll barely remember me after the change...Let alone worry for my well-being." Turning toward the main room of the cottage, she left the dim, cramped bedroom without a glance back at her broken twin.

The door to their shanty groaned in feeble protest, as she swung it back on its rusted hinges. A sudden, autumn wind picked up as Anna stepped out onto the makeshift stoop. Eyes narrowed, she stared at the slat board storage shed, tucked against the nearby tree line of pine and fir.

The dark, towering trees swayed in the late-afternoon breeze, brushing the roof of the shack. As Anna drew closer, she could hear the muted groans of the worn, cedar boards. She drew the dagger as her hand fell on the shed door, feeling little comfort from the weapon.

As she worked the rusted wire away from the corroded hasp for the second time that day, faint, guttural and anxious whispers came from within. Her fist tightened on the haft of the blade, as the crumbling cable slid from the lock and fell to the dirt at her feet. Anna dug her nails into the soft wood, and heaved the entrance open.

Inside, weak shafts of deep golden light poured through the gaps in the faded, uneven walls. Fat motes of pollen and dust floated in the thick air. And nestled in a gloomy corner, avoided by the amber sunbeams, was the Queen.

She went by many names; Queen of the Otherworld, Lady of the Dead, but her station remained constant. She was the consort of the Oak King, Lord of Abundance and Bounty. She was the dark to his light. He was the day to her night. For as long as the Wise Women had existed in the secret valley, they had been taught to respect this balance of Woodland Royalty. But Claire's dalliance, and subsequent obsession, with the Oak King, now threatened to shatter this natural equilibrium.

Queen of Samhain

The Queen stood, unfurling her long, bluish-grey body as she stepped from the shadows. Anna stepped back and watched her slip, with unnatural grace, toward the center of the storage hut. Streaks of dusty-blue mold grew in the hollows of her sharp cheeks, and down the length of her spidery arms and legs. Fat, wormy branches of orange lichen sprouted from her scalp, and fell over her shoulders in a vivid, straggly carpet. Her eyes were wide, opaque toadstools of black. Their thick, dark caps fluttered with silent anger, shooting pebble spores that floated to the dirt floor and wriggled through the hard earth, burying themselves quickly. She was an organic universe, and Anna regarded her with quiet awe. Never, on the other side of the wooden walls of the shack, speaking with this Wood Nymph in the early morn, had she expected such odd, frightening, yet strangely ethereal otherworld beauty.

Anna's eyes dropped to the heavy, iron shackles encircling the Queen's slender, fungal wrists and ankles. Her gaze followed the lengths of chains to a fat, long spike hammered into the ground, near the farthest corner of the shed.

Anna lowered to her haunches, placing the dagger and basin before her, just beyond the reach of the wood spirit. "I should set you free."

The forest monarch nodded. "You should, but you won't."

Anna frowned as the lithe, wood wisp cocked her head and gave a vague, smug smile. "Perhaps I will let you go. I could deny Claire her foolish wish. The wasting will bring death to her soon, I am sure. Her mad infatuation would end, and I would have peace of mind."

The Queen knelt in front of her, and skulked closer on all four, spongy limbs. "Aye, that would be wise."

Anna gathered the bowl and weapon into her lap and scrambled back. The lengths of chain appeared to grow, and the Queen's mossy fingers brushed up against her leg.

"But tell me, witch woman, what will make your heart ache more?" She tossed her head, and her slimy curls squirmed like slugs as they brushed across the earthen floor. "To watch your beloved twin slowly die, or to spill the blood of a forest nymph you despise?"

Anna shimmied away from the touch of her cold, rapid breath. "I do not despise you. I respect the balance your kind maintains, and the code that stands between our people."

A low, raspy cackle came from the Queen. "If you truly valued these tenets you speak of, you would not be here now, brandishing a knife and ready to pierce my heart."

Anna's hands fell from her lap, and her tools of sacrifice tumbled onto the packed dirt between them. "Why is it I cannot deny Claire? I cannot fathom the punishment that will answer this horrible crime of mine, yet I am driven to commit it for her." She cried into her open palms.

"Do not grieve, child." The Queen's rough, velvet touch caressed her neck, and she shivered. "Perhaps the Oak King was enticed as much by your sister, as she was bewitched by him. I think we both know Claire has been practicing the black arts far longer than she will admit. Her beguiling ways have caught up with her."

"Still, I must try to save her, wretched though she may be." The smell of rotting pumpkins filled her nostrils, as Anna gathered up the dagger and basin and slowly stood.

Slinking back into her shadowed corner, the Queen nodded sagely. "Just remember, witch, balance always finds a way to restore itself. What happens now, don't mistake, it was meant to happen. The Curse of Goddard ran far deeper with its taint than we, the Fae Folk, sensed, admitted. What needs to be done, we have ignored for far too long. Cleansing...we knew it then, long ago, but we chose to ignore it, hoped his discarnate spite would wither and fade, or pass to the Summerlands..."

A calm coldness spread through her body, and Anna plunged forward into the deep murk where the forest nymph waited, as the Queen's words faded into nothingness. She went with eyes closed, letting her intuition guide her. She clutched the dirk with hands that felt awkward and young.

There came a low, sinister laugh to her left, and then her right. Coarse, icy palms cupped her neck, and a murmured chorus of jumbled words seeped into her mind. Anna concentrated on shutting out the distracting glamour. Her fingers itched against the blade.

She hollered out as she whirled around and lunged forward. The dagger found its mark and there was a wet, ripping sound. Black blood jutted from the ragged tear in the center of the Queen's chest, spraying the front of Anna's apron. The wood wisp shuttered, and a weak moan gurgled up from her throat. She staggered back, and slumped into a pile of soft, spoiled pumpkins from the final harvest.

Anna dropped her weapon. Quiet tears spilled down her cheeks as she skittered to the corpse, jabbing the basin beneath the wound with shaky hands. "Forgive me." She looked into the pool of dark liquid collected, and then backed away from the fallen Fae.

The shack door slammed shut behind her as she left. Anna jumped, letting out a tiny yelp. The ebony fluid sloshed dangerously close to the edge of the bowl, and she stopped to steady her grip. The moon's silver light reflected off the murky pool, and she stared at its wavering image.

How did so much time pass? she wondered. The small hairs on the back of her neck stood on end. She could not have been more than half an hour in the shed. Anna was sure of that, yet three hours of daylight had somehow slipped away. The full Samhain moon rose high over the silhouette of the distant mountains.

She pulled her attention away from the deepening, indigo sky and picked up her pace, casting a nervous glance behind her as she scampered toward the cabin. The dirt crunched beneath her feet as she drew closer, echoing like thunder in her ears.

The tip of her buttoned boot touched the porch platform as the earth beneath her trembled, and a deep rumbling came from behind her. Anna clutched the full vessel tight against her midriff, and slid her foot away from the stoop.

"Wise woman, what have you done?"

Her heart froze in her chest.

"Turn and face me. You must answer for your deed."

Anna held her breath until her lungs burned, preparing herself for what was to come, and then turned.

"Lift your head. I must judge your callous act by the guilt in your eyes."

Anna obeyed, taking in the looming presence of the Oak King. His yellow, hawkish glare bore into her. His pale, Oak-bark brows were drawn together in a frown of bitter sadness.

His massive, tree trunk legs brought him a step nearer. He cocked his head, and his fuzz dappled antlers traced willowy shadows across the ground in front of her, as they played with the climbing moonlight.

Anna's eyes dropped to his snaky, clubbed feet, and she followed the trail of his white, wide roots with her gaze. They disappeared into a large, jagged hole behind him. Beyond the lip of this chasm, she spied a set of earthen stairs leading down into the underworld.

"You have killed my consort." The words came out impassive, but she could feel the acrid despair that haunted his undertone. "The consequences will be great."

Her response caught in her throat, strangled by the gnarled barbs of fear. Anna dropped her head and folded her hands low against her waist. "What will you do to Claire?"

He laughed and stepped closer, wrapping his smooth, icy palm around her shoulder. "Always concern for your sister, yet what care has she for you? You've come to commit her crime, despite the danger it has put you in."

Through the thick fabric of her dress, her skin tingled beneath his touch. A deep, distant pain gnawed inside her arm, spreading up her neck and down her side.

"Still, you both must pay if the balance of the forest is to be restored."

Anna tried to cry out, but nothing came. She tried to flee, but the Wood Man ensnared her wrist in a feathery, branchlike grip, pulling her tight against his chest.

"A life in exchange for a life." His thorny fingernails dug into her arm, "That is how it is with the forest people. The dead must rise tonight, attended by the Oak King and his Queen. They shall walk among the living this Samhain, as they have since time forgotten."

"Then I must get the Queen's blood to Claire." She struggled to lift her face from his clammy skin. In a slow, dreamy instant, she realized her hands were empty and wet. Somehow, she had dropped the vital life fluid.

"It is not that simple, I am afraid. Your sister must be punished, not rewarded." The forest ruler took her chin in his hand. "Besides, my love, are your lips not already stained with the essence of my departed lady?"

His voice came through a haze, and Anna raised her fingertips to her numbed lips. They came away wet and sticky, and an unpleasant fire throbbed in her mouth.

"You," she closed her eyes, and her head spun with a fog of frantic thought, "tricked me."

An absent tickling crawled over her scalp, and she dug her fingers into her thick knot of hair. Her hand came away with scraps of moist flesh and russet curls clinging to it.

"What are you doing to me?" Anna was disconnected from the pain, and her question seemed to come from the lips of another.

"The change will not take long." The Oak King pushed her back from him, but held fast to her arms. A wide, long-toothed grin spread across his angular face. "Be patient."

There was a soft *pop*, and Anna's ruined eyes dribbled down her cheeks. All went black for a moment, until jet toadstools sprouted from her emptied sockets, and she saw with the preternatural vision of a wood wisp. Something damp and coarse slithered down her neck, and slippery limbs of lichen burrowed underneath her dress, tearing the starched material away from her reshaped form.

"Can you walk, my lady?"

Whispers filled her head as he lifted her into his smooth, large arms. The cool breath of the dead brushed against Anna's newly transformed body, as the Oak King carried her down the crumbling stairwell and into the fissure.

Where are you going? The protest drifted into her head, but it came weak, and almost alien, to the Queen. *What are you doing, Anna?*

In her mind, the nymph watched as Claire sat up in bed, eyes wide with panic.

The Queen wrapped her newborn, moldy arms around the corded neck of her consort. "What fate awaits her, my lord?"

He kissed her pointed chin. "She will forever waste away, crippled by her mad infatuation until her body turns into a living corpse."

She rested her head against his collarbone. "It is befitting of her transgression."

They entered a corridor of clay, and phantom limbs reached out from their loamy tombs to stroke the face of the Queen, welcoming her. She brushed their wispy fingers across her lips and smiled.

"Come," the King ducked beneath a low archway, and they entered a vast, murky chamber, "let us prepare for our ascension."

The dead sighed in anxious agreement.

They Are Bound...Not Frozen
John Dimes

Ora glanced down at her lap for the directions she printed out from *MapQuest*. She hoped to god that the information was at least up to date, if not expediently direct. She'd prefer, for a change, to turn down a road, or to take an exit that actually still existed. Though the countryside was beautiful, Ora felt that at any second, the pastoral back roads of Hanover would inexplicably change from a main thoroughfare to a dead end cul-de-sac.

"Cocoa. *Chuh–chuh–chocolate.* It breaks the bonds. *It breaks the bonds.* Eh–it frees us. . . ." her boyfriend chattered in his sleep.

Ora turned the heater on as far as it would go, but it did little to dampen the unearthly chill that poured forth from the backseat, and eerily pervaded the car. She watched her slumbering boyfriend from the rearview as he continued to mumble in that anguished, discomfiting warble that she was most certainly tired of hearing. She wanted to put this, and the affairs of the night before, behind her. More importantly, she wanted to reclaim the health and sanity of her boyfriend, Zan. But to achieve this end, she had to travel ahead, and confront a man about imprisoned souls.

-SOH-

Zan checked his watch expectantly: 10:20.
They should've delivered it by now.
Zan Delano was the twenty-eight year old proprietor of Shantz Diner, one of those small, quiet neighborhood establishments that catered to colorful locals who liked their food simple, and their company sociable. Though situated near a busy main street of pricey restaurants, malls brimming with expensive retailers, and tiny art house/multiplex theaters, Shantz somehow managed to maintain its air of nouveau, and not-so-nouveau, poor exclusivity.

When Zan took over the reign of ownership from the eighty-two year old retiree, Noah Shantz, he had to promise certain standards would be maintained, otherwise no sale. Mind you, most of Shantz's final directives were not conveyed in a manner resembling those of the elder statesmen to the snot-nosed brat; the ideas were expressed as though the two were more or less equals. Shantz had Zan in his employ since the boy arrived to the area with his mother when he was just seventeen. During that time, an unexpected grooming of the young man had taken place.

Shantz's Directives:

Priority #1: "People come here like their fries twice cooked," Shantz said. "Fry 'em up at the beginning of the day. Leave 'em sittin' there under that there light until some old lady cries arthritis. When folks order a batch, dump 'em under the grease again. Salt. Pepper. Ketchup. Not *catsup*. Catsup is sweet."

Priority #2: "Never, ever get rid of the signature dish! To wit, the ten for a dollar 'OK Burgers.' "

Zan recalled the neighborhood favorite, so named because of the burger's ability to fit neatly in the hollow of one's index finger curled into the thumb. One could have whatever one wanted on the "OK Burger", but it had to be pretty sparse, due to the obvious lack of playing surface. Usually it was served with mustard, ketchup, and cat dander confetti of diced onions.

Priority #3: "Jimmy Kelly," Zan remembered Shantz to say, "He's like a lot of folks that come in here for a strong cup. *A strong cup.* Dump what seems ta be half a kilo in the filter. Make level sure that every molecule of water has been occupied with the notion of becoming a sludge that keeps folks jittery for hours!

"You don't do that, folks like Kelly will likely grouse about how much better their wives, or mothers make it! You'll wanna kill'em by the end of it."

Priority #4, the most important one: "This place may not mean much to you at times, or it could mean too much, but be happy with yourself first and foremost, the rest'll take care of itself. Know what I mean?"

"Sure, sure," Zan said.

A handshake and a signed loan contract from the local Mercantile Bank later, and Shantz was happily his. And he was determined to keep his word with Shantz. . . .*but with only one proviso. . .*

John Dimes

He wanted an ice cream machine.

-SOH-

A large white truck without any markings pulled into the diner's parking lot, which effectively obscured the morning light that poured in from the front window.

10:32. *Almost on time*, Zan thought.

Zan saw this stripe-shirted fellow who had to be at least seven, or eight years younger than himself, scrawny and spiked hair, as he awkwardly emerged from the truck.

The boy leaned in to talk to his partner who remained in the truck.

Scrawny Spiked Hair checked his tablet. Satisfied that he was at the right place, he came in.

"Uh, hi! Hi. Um, I'm looking for the owner, Zan Delano?"

"Yeah, I'm *Zon*," he said as he came around the counter.

The kid sized up the situation. Came up impressed. "Zon? Kewl, kewl. Where do you want us to bring it through?"

"The front is fine, I think."

While the kid worked up the paperwork for Zan to sign, he gave the kid a quick once over. He took pity on the unfortunate looking young man, with his crude islands of acne-reddened skin. And his smile: It unsteadied Zan as he examined the boy's mouth, which was practically caramelized by an obvious—or not so obvious to the uninitiated—Crystal Meth habit. Zan was sweaty all-the-sudden and overwhelmed with a need to vomit.

"Mr. Delano? You alright?" the boy asked, in response to Zan's sickly expression.

"Uh, I'm alright, I–I guess," he couldn't tear his eyes away from the boy's mouth. More precisely—his teeth.

Self-consciously, Scrawny Spiked Hair covered his mouth. "Um, here's your paperwork," he said, tight-lipped.

And with papers signed, the kid and his partner struggled with an oversized box, through an entrance that was rail-thin in comparison, with rumbling that threatened to shatter the front window.

With the image of the boy's mouth emblazoned upon his mind's eye, he reflected on a previous instance when he experienced the same type of nausea.

It was two months prior to the arrival of his precious cargo. Zan had attended the Food Service Conference in Toronto to make a few possible industry contacts.

For the most part, tables were attended by interested business types eager to hear what a company had to offer. But for those dismal few customer reps that hadn't a soul standing before them, well, they'd start licking their lips, it seemed, as they achieved a sort of desperate, predatory gleam to their eye that made Zan look away uncomfortably. Inwardly, he laughed at how much of a timid little girl he was about confrontation.

Telemarketers, he thought.

Zan could never hang up on telemarketers. He always left that up to Ora, his beautiful, yet occasionally uncouth, roughneck "sistah" of a girlfriend.

"Telemarketer, huh?" he'd recalled her asking in

response to his look of helpless silence.

"Baby, why do you keep sparing those people's feelings like you know them or something?" she'd say, or some version like it, while she plucked the receiver away from his comically startled face, so to let the one-sided conversation climax to its inevitable, and abrupt end.

"Rejection," she said, dropping the receiver with a dull clatter, "is implied in their job description, I'm quite sure."

His "honey brown baby" was always good for closure.

So, with his girlfriend's strength in mind, Zan gave any exceedingly industrious vendors a wide berth, because he was damned if he was going to be muscled into a major purchase simply out of pity for a salesman and a time honored pitch.

Zan ventured away from the distractions of the convention floor center, and pushed through towards the fringes where his original goal laid, *the industrial ice cream makers*, and he safely stumbled into the proximity of a retinue of friendly individuals, handing out free ice cream samples. Proudly he made the rounds, ingesting whatever frozen confection was pushed at him. In time he graduated from small, urine sample portions, to larger fares, where he found himself gleefully nibbling at the cold, sweet edges of a waffle cone, topped with a mound of vanilla, sprinkled with crushed nuts.

While Zan nursed at his cone of ice cream, he came upon a pair of machines that set his brain to sweating. He bore silent witness to a pair of Coldelite-Carpigiani Soft Serve Ice Cream Machines. One served double flavored twists, and the other, single serve. The single service machine, he recalled from a catalogue, was priced at an affordable $6888.00, as opposed to its brother, which was an easy ten grand.

"They are beautiful, aren't they?" asked a woman.

Zan hadn't realized time had passed until he noticed there was melted ice cream running over his knuckles.

"Yes, yes they are," agreed Zan.

"We've come a long way from the 'Carvelis: 'No Air Pump, Super-Low Temperature, Soft Serve System.'"

Zan was impressed. "Uh, yeah. Yeah. Yeah we have."

"Which do you prefer out of the two, then?"

"Well. . . .well, the C.C. Double twist machine over there cost about ten grand. Now, some folks are pretty particular about their swirl. I figure for six grand, I'd get the C.C. Single, and tell those folks just to get over it. So I—" He caught himself suddenly. "Are you a salespers—?"

"Oh, no, nonono. Well," she laughed. "I am. I-I, uh, not for this company. I'm with another vendor."

Zan did a quick scan of her vendor badge. It read: *HaloGen, Inc.*

"Your company sells, um, lightbulbs and stuff? Lighting accessories?"

The woman rolled her eyes, comically. "It's pronounced HALO-gen. Halo, as in, well, *angels*. And Gen, which is short for *Genesis*."

"Sorry. Didn't realize." Zan hoped to god that the woman wasn't, well. . . .working for, or in the name of, God. If so, he really had to figure out how to politely pry loose. He *was* susceptible to remorseful passivity, after all.

"It's fine. I've gotten that a lot today. We're actually an ice cream manufacturer, very new to the market. Are you a retailer?"

"Uh, I own my own restaurant. Well, it's a diner

really," he said, somewhat apologetically.

"Ah, an entrepreneur! And so young! Oh, that's good. That's very good," assured the woman, genuinely. "The world gets tired of its Burger Kings, and its McDonalds. Occasionally we need a more human touch, don't you find? A single mind behind everything—actually there on site—*on the premises*, instead of an ineffectual gestalt, or committee of minds headquartered hundreds of miles away, deciding every little thing!"

"Yeah, yeah! That's right. Totally right."

Zan mentally leapt back and finally considered what he had in front of him for. The lady was what his ragtag band of friends would've described as a "MILF": *A Mom I'd Like to Fuck.* Indeed, she was an attractive "forty-something" woman with a close, thick crowd of brunette curls, high cheek bones, and piercing cerulean blue eyes. Though dressed conservatively in a suit of brown tweed, her pomegranate blouse gave an altogether different impression. There was as a tight line of cleavage to be had, and a complimentary fullness of form that was undeniably distracting.

"Listen, you—you say you're with an ice cream

manufacturer?" he asked.

"Yes, yes I did. Ice cream and accessories. We're currently looking for enterprising people like you to partner with."

Zan cycled the statement in his head. Arrived at the *proper* conclusion in seconds.

"Have any, uh, free samples?"

The lady smiled. Her teeth were fashion model perfect, glistening with the sheen of freshly cooked orzo.

"Of course I do, um—" she checked his visitor badge. "Zan, is it?" asked the woman.

"Actually it's Zon, as in VerraZANo. Zan makes it a little less 'old world,'" he said.

"Right!" She laughed. "Well, I'm Ross. Ross Kilmer. Pleased to make your acquaintance."

In no time at all, Zan and Ms. Kilmer were out of the convention space, into the adjacent corridors where the smaller auditoriums lay. They arrived at the auditorium with the placard that read: **HaloGen**.

At this point, a strong fragrance hit him.

"Wow! That smells good. What is it?"

"Our new line of iced confections: *Brozia*," Ms. Kilmer explained.

"Like in, um, *Ambrosia*, the, nectar of the gods?"

"Yes, that's right, exactly!" she said, as she ushered Zan into the auditorium with a dramatic flourish.

Once inside, Zan noticed the disparity in the chair to attendance ratio. Along with him, there were nine other men in attendance who were gathered on stage around a 30 x 40 rectangle of silver, churning with what appeared to be a huge vat of ice cream.

"*Brozia*," she said as they ventured down the isle of the auditorium, towards the stage, "is an all natural extract, processed with a state of the art freezing technique involving the de-vitrification of ice particles, where water particles, frozen water crystals, are essentially stripped away, resulting in a heightened clarity of flavor, and an extreme abundance of aroma."

Zan couldn't have agreed more. "Wow!" He breathed in the exotic aroma that held the intensity of powdery, spiced incense, edged with a kind of citrus tang. It amazed him that he was salivating, given the fact that within the last half hour, he had more than consumed his own body weight in junk food freebies.

They Are Bound...Not Frozen

On stage, Zan and Kilmer were approached by a husky gentleman in his mid-fifties. He reflexively fastened the top bottom of his ancient green blazer then, thought better of it as his belly protruded past the suit's intended sartorial limits.

"Hello, I'm Kenneth Hadley," he said as he shook Zan's hand.

"Zan Delano."

"Want to try a cup of *Brozia,* or would you much rather read literature on it beforehand?" asked Hadley, good-naturedly.

"Oh, quit tcasing the boy, Hadley! Give 'em a dish already!" urged a gentleman who stood out of from the rest of the suit-wearing attendees, like the proverbial sore thumb.

He was a balding, older, heavyset gent, simply attired in jeans, and an untucked long sleeve shirt, featuring a vividly designed serpent skull on a black background, complete with a dagger impaled heart across the tongue of his left pocket. Zan took note of the man's name immediately.

"What *Bart* said," said Zan.

Someone handed Zan a saucer of *Brozia.* It was a slimly built man, who appeared of Mediterranean

114

descent with his jet waves, burnished olive complexion, and aquiline nose. He wore a remarkably stylish cranberry bespoke suit. Zan had cousins like this guy. Cousins that often teased him on his wholesome, "white boy next door" good looks. Justin Timberlake, they'd call him. He didn't deny the resemblance, though he hoped he at least appeared somewhat mentally alert.

It surprised him that his obviously moneyed "cousin" should be serving up a dish of cream to a bunch of freeloaders in cheap suits.

"Careful now kid," cautioned Bart, comically. His spoon of *Brozia* poised in mid taste. "Stuff is loaded with preservatives! You ain't old enough to remember it, but Red Dye #2 used ta cause cancer in laboratory animals!"

"Mr. Simms!" Ms. Kilmer playfully scolded, as she drew the man aside for a more private discussion.

Zan eagerly molded his lips around the spoon, taking in the *Brozia's* flavor. Its brief cologne stunningly resonated in his throat and nostrils. His posture, his general well-being, gradually changed, it seemed, due to the potent quality of the *Brozia* startling his senses in the nicest sort of way.

"What's this? This stuff have alcohol?" he asked.

"*Brozia* is non-narcotic. Non-alcoholic," explained Hadley. "You're experiencing a gradual release of endorphins, another property inherent of the extracts. As I'm sure Ms. Kilmer told you, our patented process gets right to the heart of the vitamins and nutrients necessary for proper brain functioning. No negative after effects. None of the 'crash' attributed to caffeinated_sodas or energy drinks."

"Come in any other flavors?" Zan asked.

"Strawberry, vanilla, or it can be eaten just so," said Hadley.

"No chocolate?"

Hadley glowered a bit at Zan's silent, well-dressed, "cousin."

"Well, we're still working on the formula for that. But rest assured—" said Hadley.

"Listen, I really think I can do well with this stuff in my shop. But you really have to make it worth my while. People like chocolate. I love chocolate. I was counting on making chocolate shakes. I mean, I'm already losing customers to Wendy's and their

Chocolate Frosties as is." That wasn't a lie, necessarily. Just business prevarication, Zan thought.

Still, he eyed up the industrial ice cream machine like it was one of Ms. Kilmer's mechanized siblings. The raised stenciling along the machine's tempered glass lid read: **Xenon Gelus 300**. He retained some minor stats about the machine, ingredient capacities and such, but didn't bother to commit it to memory out of simple financial necessity.

"That's a fine piece of equipment," Hadley said, as he favored the young man with a knowing expression.

"Yes. Yes it is."

A quiet smile passed between he and Hadley, and an agreement of sorts was tacitly reached.

Zan caught his well dressed "cousin" smiling from the corner of his eye. He wondered, was it the lighting, or just plain fatigue, that made the man's teeth resemble mottled kernels of Indian corn.

Zan randomly trained his focus across the various faces in the room. For some reason, he had a strange preoccupation with everyone's mouths. He saw nothing particularly unusual until he reached

Ms. Kilmer. Previously her smile, more precisely, her teeth, seemed like a harmonious affiliation of perfectly set cuspids and molars. Now it seemed her smile shimmered too harshly, that her teeth were being gradually consumed, or enveloped within a presence of thick shadows.

-SOH-

Zan wearily trudged into his apartment at 2:30am. A month and a half of amazing business had consistently kept his schedule later and later. His greasy signature dishes continued to fly off the grill. But nothing performed so well as his sweet, sweet *Brozia.* Everybody but everybody wanted *Brozia.*

"Two Strawberry Brozia's please!"

"Gimme mine just so."

And the perpetual: *"Dude , when are you going to carry chocolate?"*

He'd queried *HaloGen* with that very question several times over the weeks, and was given the "still working on it" routine. An answer that Zan had gotten tired of hearing. It wasn't cutting into his business, necessarily. But it wasn't increasing it either.

So he decided to take matters into his own hands, by making a last minute purchase from an all night grocery.

He sat the plastic bag on the kitchen table then decided to check on his girlfriend. He knew she wouldn't wait up for him, but it would've been nice to see a book folded in her lap, or the TV on as evidence of her struggle to try. And as expected, he heard only silence as he approached the bedroom. There wasn't a book in sight. Ora was curled beneath the covers, dead to the world.

He was overwhelmed by what he deemed as "Corn Devotion," as he inwardly remarked on how hot a number she was, even asleep. He also thought he better resist that urge to land a kiss on the warm shadows of her sienna colored cheeks. Though well intentioned, it would've only amounted to:

"Have you lost your goddamn mind? Not everybody got their own business! I got to work tomorrow!" So on and so forth.

Poor thing needed all the restful mental stamina she could muster. Work as a dental assistant/hygienist wasn't an easy thing. She often swore that during "routine" cleanings, patients sneaked bites of food while her head was turned.

Let her sleep. Let her sleep.

-SOH-

In the kitchen, Zan triumphantly produced his chocolate syrup from the plastic bag. It wasn't Hershey's, but it was the best he could find on short notice. He got the container of *Brozia* from the freezer and hunted for a spoon. He ripped the plastic safety seal from the chocolate bottle with his teeth. He used his teeth for the lid as well. He liberally coated the *Brozia* with chocolate. With everything in place, he sat against the edge of the counter and gulped down a mouth full of cream.

"Not bad," he thought.

He experienced that same stunning sensation in his head, an almost euphoric submission into the cold, calming influence of the *Brozia's* pungent aroma. He also experienced other more unfamiliar sensations as well, as his body gradually lost sense of itself, as though it had become weightless.

John Dimes

Ephemeral.

A tide of nausea quickly rolled in on his belly, and his head ached sharply as images invaded his mind. Visions of a myriad of floating bodies beneath the murky waves of a treacly sea. Of bones bursting from the bloody husks of lifeless flesh, the sound of tearing skin crackling harshly against his ears. Any thoughts of drowning beneath such grisly mire were quickly erased by the stench that rose against his nostrils, replacing the sweet scent of the *Brozia*.

Translucent shapes swam past his vision then. Outlines of bodies. Zan's eyes adjusted to the gloom, and he realized that the waters themselves were the translucent beings. That they were the medium in which he swam. They rushed at him like anxious minnow, invisibly clawing at his face. Prying his lips apart. He frantically thrashed about as the hands scrambled into his mouth. He felt a dull, painless tugging as they worried his teeth loose from his gums. Pellets of coagulated blood launched sluggishly from his lips, and trailed to their faces, as each being cupped their hands to their own mouths. . . .*partaking of a single tooth.* The concrete imagery of his individual teeth stood in stark contrast against all those immaterial jaw lines and ruined palates.

While the beings silently regarded Zan, the scene changed. Ice formations fractured and crashed in upon them. The beings, as a body, howled with a force that buffeted Zan about like a hapless piece of timber.

-SOH-

Zan came to with a start.

"You all right?" Ora asked.

His girlfriend was kneeling over him, daubing his head with a wet dish towel.

He sat himself up from the floor and saw that the kitchen splattered with chocolate. It was even on his person. His mouth was smeared with it. He was surprised to find remnants of it leaking from his nostrils. Ora brought the dish towel up to his face again, and dutifully wiped away as much as she could.

"What the hell happ—"

Ora errantly tossed the cloth aside. Got to a chair. Composed herself. "I asked you, *are you okay?*"

"Yeah. Yeah, I'm all right. It was just a bad dream, I think."

"What the fuck of?"

Normally he forgot his dreams immediately upon waking. He didn't have to think long on this one, though. It was all still very fresh.

"Uh,uhum. . . .I don't know. All these people. Dead people, I guess. I was . . . I was swimming inside them like, like they were water, or something. And—you'll like this one. . . they were pulling my teeth."

"Say what?"

"They were taking my teeth, and putting them in their own mouths."

Ora stared at him mystified.

"Did I puke myself or something?" Zan asked, touching his clothes.

"You did a damn sight more than that! You—" she was lost for words, suddenly.

"Baby, I—I came in here, and you were jerking around on the floor like you were having a seizure, or something. Was gonna call 911. Get you to an emergency room. I thought it was alcohol poisoning. Food poisoning. Some kind of allergic reaction or something," she said wearily. "But, then . . . then stuff, stuff started happening.

"You started vomiting. But what you vomited," she had to really ponder how to properly phrase it. "What you vomited. . . .*stood up.*"

Zan was perplexed. "Stood up? What do you mean *'stood up?'*"

She shakily performed her little pantomime. Silently. Dramatically. Haughtily, she rose from her chair. Moved about *"easy-as- you-please"*. Resumed her seat.

"You got to be kidding."

She shook her head "no" that she wasn't.

"But—"

"Honey, I work around teeth all day," she said. "It gets to a point you start dreaming about them.

"You know my folks? My people? We're big on dream dictionaries. You've seen me with them. Dream about money? Then you better play the numbers tomorrow. That kind of stuff. Now, when I have dreams about teeth falling out, it don't mean much. I'm seeing teeth ready to fall out of people's faces all day. But you, when you start having dreams about teeth falling out? That means something! Especially with all that shit that flew up out of your face, like—like. . .? "

"Baby!" Zan was frightened. "What does it generally mean?"

"When your teeth fall out?" Ora asked. "Bad news. Death to someone close to you. But. . . but that doesn't seem right, somehow. I think—"

"Go ahead."

"It's all obviously tied together. That stuff on the floor there. What you dreamed," she said. "What did you say? There were dead people coming at you? Taking something from you?"

"Yeah."

"Did they look angry or pleased afterwards?"

Zan laughed. "I—I was actually too goddamn scared to pay attention, really."

Ora offered a half hearted smile. "Fine. But, did they say anything to you? Or at least try?"

"Well, they *looked* like they wanted to say something. But everything changed."

"Changed? Changed how?"

"Ice. Everything was covered in ice."

Ora shook her head in mild disbelief, while she rang her pretty young hands like some old crone.

"Lord, lord, lord!   Listen to enough ghost stories, and you start living one yourself!"

He scooted over to her, took her hands in his.

"Relax, baby. Relax. What do you got?"

"I know you're not into monster movies, ghost stories, and stuff. But the stuff I've heard, and read about spiritualists, or metaphysicians, whatever you want to call'em. Dead folks, they say, can come off acting pretty random. Others are more specific. The more specific ones, in order to communicate to the living, tend to take something that's necessary to the task, be it physical, or well. . ." she had to say it. ". . . Psychic."

"Um, like teeth?"

"Or the tongue. Anything to do with the mouth. It's, um, um, what they call, mostly *symbolic.* "

Zan took a deep breath while he attempted to massage the initial pangs of a migraine from his head.

"Baby, I highly suggest—*highly suggest*—you find out what the fuck is goin' on with that ice cream of yours," she said, in her "no nonsense" tone.

"There's nothing I can do about it now. In the morning I'll—*huhAAAAAAAH*!"

John Dimes

"Zon!"

Something like a razor bit into his mind. "Just a headache. . . n—need to rest. *Nuhaaaahh. . .*"

Zan passed out. While under, he thought he heard the sound of his own voice speaking in a curious, rapid fire succession.

"Prettygirlprettygirlprettygirlprettygirl, ohyesohyesohyes–hnnnnn. . . . ."

His inflections on certain words were off, somehow.

". . . .noheavennohell,noheaven, onlycold. Socoldsocoldsocoldsocold–hnnnnnn. . . ."

His pitch was higher, too. He could hear the strain on his throat as it coaxed out its uncomfortable alto.

"Zan? What's—?" he heard Ora call.

"HnnnnnnnNotnotnotnotnot. . . .nonono--not ZannnnnnnnnUHHHhhhhhhnnnnn," he heard himself say.

"Kelly, Edith Kelly. Kelly, Edith Kelly. Kelly, I'm, I'm, I-I-I! ME! I'm–I'm, Eh. . .Edith–Edith— Eduhthnnnnn. . ."

From time to time Zan would come to and he'd see Ora's anxious face. She'd be speaking to him.

They Are Bound...Not Frozen

Her tentative words coming at him in soft, erratic waves, where words were formed and produced moments later.

-SOH-

Ora looked at Zan through the rearview mirror. He had been restive in sleep most of the trip. She noticed that he stirred and wearily surveyed his surroundings.

"Throat's sore," he said hoarsely. "Felt like I was screaming all night."

She smiled at him through the rearview. "Actually you were pretty talkative."

"Really? I don't remember."

"You wouldn't," she said, enigmatically.

"What–what did I miss? Where are we?"

"We're in Pennsylvania," said Ora, matter-of-fact.

They reached a fork. Veered right.

"What the hell?" Zan stretched a bit. Yawned. "Why—?"

"We're on an errand. Just go back to sleep, baby. I'll wake you when we get there."

"Okay," he said, like an unusually obedient child,

as he curled up to sleep.

Ora wondered if her life could her get any weirder than last night. Seeing her boyfriend being, well, possessed by some strange entity.

At first she thought Zan was just putting her on. But the smell that came off of him wasn't right. His usual pheromonal output—a mild kind of masculine, first wave, salt sweat musk—would unconsciously, and consciously (*very consciously*), get her randy for all sorts of activities. However, at the time, she found herself totally put off by the odor that breathed off of him. It was the scent of cold *Brozia* gone sour.

And that voice that spoke through him. The poor creature's train of thought was not an easy thing to follow, as it jumped from subject to subject. To Ora's mind, the experience was like playing Double Dutch, where one had to time oneself precisely so as not to get snagged in the turning jump ropes.

"Who are you?" Ora recalled asking.

"Kelly, Edith Kelly. Kelly, Edith Kelly. KELL—"

"Calm down, now. Calm down. What...what do you want?"

"Inainanaina, in a cage! Frozenwithbodies. A-allthosebodies.   Frozenfrozenfrozen.

They Are Bound...Not Frozen

Deadthingssurroundingmeahaannnnnnnn!
Touchingme! End! End, thoughtthoughtswouldstop.
Wouldsleepwouldsleephnnnnnnn. . .!"

"Please. Please, slow down. I don't understand."

Edith, the woman who spoke through Zan,
composed herself as best she could. "Was...was
awake in, in, in. That place. I–hahhhhnnnnn. . . "

"What place?"

"Gen? Gen? GEN! Gen? Gengengengengen. . . "

"HaloGen?"

The creature's face was turned in confusion. Ora
sadly looked on at her boyfriend, who she knew
wasn't her boyfriend. He was just a puppet,
animated by the creature.

Ora was close to tears.

The being inhaled suddenly. "Cry? CRY!
CRYCRYCRYCRYCRY!!!!" it exclaimed in frustration.

Ora feebly offered a sympathetic gaze. "I know, I
know. I feeling like crying too."

The creature inhaled again. "CRYcrycry, Oh,
gengengengenhnnnnnnnn. . ."

The being seemed to lose all reason at that point,
and babbled on incomprehensibly, like some
schizophrenic street person. After about twenty

minutes of listening to the being's fitful rants, Ora decided that sleeping pills were in order. Finding that they were out, she got out the "non-drowsy formula" allergy medicine, fed it to Zan, and he. . .they. . . .finally slept.

Ora went through Zan's papers and found a letter with HaloGen's masthead. There was a phone number, and a P.O. Box, but no actual street address. She then went to the computer. Did an online search for HaloGen, then, did another search for a company called *CryoGen.* There she learned more about cryogenics, more precisely, *cryonics,* than she ever really wanted to know. From the chemicals they used to treat the bodies for freezing, to the storage units in which the bodies were placed. There was something called a "Bigfoot" freezing unit, an enormous liquid nitrogen filled canister that could contain up to four whole bodies at a time, with sufficient space for five *disembodied* heads. These heads were apparently prepped for Neuropreservation, where at a future time, when science would be equipped to the task, they would unite these heads with healthy, cloned bodies.

Suitably alarmed, and repulsed, she took a quick

scroll down to the bottom of all the graphs and statistics, and found something that did not unduly surprise her: That *CryoGen* and *HaloGen* were located in the same area.

-SOH-

The car rattled up the gravel road and pulled into a small lot, situated a few yards from the unassuming, two story office facility that was CryoGen Incorporated—which was quietly set out in the middle of a pleasant tract of nowhere. Ora parked beside one of the only two cars in the lot.

After checking on her quietly dozing boyfriend, she got out, and made for the building. There were two sets of stairs facing on either sides of the building. She decided to head up right. As luck would have it, she found the main office almost immediately.

A young lady was slipping on her coat, as she suddenly emerged from the doorway.

"Ooh!" she yelped.

"I'm sorry! I'm sorry!" said Ora. "Didn't mean to startle you."

"Oh, that's okay. Um, I'm sorry. We're closed to visitors for the evening."

"Oh, that's too bad," she glanced over her shoulder at the car. "I've come a long way, actually. Got lost a couple of times, *hah*, you know? Directions were a mess!"

"I, well. . ."

"Is Dr. Hadley still in? It's really important that I talk to him."

The girl pulled her coat tighter around her.

"Yes, he is." The girl quickly wrestled with what to do. Finally: "Hm. . .let me see if he'll talk to you, okay?" she said, sweetly, as she went back inside. "Come on in. S'cold!"

"Oh, sure, sure!"

Ora followed the young lady into the calming green of the waiting room.

"I'll see if he'll talk to you," the girl said, as she moved to the door at the right of her desk. Sheepishly she knocked at the door, while entering his office.

"Thank you!" Ora smiled so hard, she thought she actually heard a muscle in her face rip. When the girl wasn't present, the rictus grin dropped suddenly, only to miraculously reappear as the girl reappeared.

"You're in luck! He'll see you," she said. "Just go right on in! Forgive me, but. . . !" The girl glanced at her watch.

"Totally understand, girl."

And with a cheerful "bye, now," the young lady was out.

Ora entered Hadley's office and saw him at his desk reviewing paperwork. He stood to greet her.

"Hello, I'm Kenneth Hadley." he extended his hand.

She didn't accept. "Forgive me. . . .dish pan hands."

"Uh, um that's fine," he said. "Please have a seat, then."

As she sat, she ruefully surveyed his office. She realized that, under different circumstances, all the awards and diplomas would inspire a great deal of trust out of an actual client.

"How may I help you, Miss. . .?"

"Wheatley," she said.

"How may I help you, Miss Wheatley?"

She stared at him hard and mean. "Recently I've

been...I've been investigating, um, cryonics. Uh, cryopreservation?"

"For yourself, or—?"

"For someone else. He hasn't been. . . doing very well."

He nodded his head, knowingly. "I...I see. Yes."

"So, I wanted to ask a few questions, if I could."

"Of course, Miss Wheatley," he said, kindly.

"Well..." Her expression grew more malevolent. "What happens to the body after freezing?"

"We don't like to think of them as bodies, but patients."

"When you say 'patients,' you mean they are not clinically dead?"

"Clinically speaking, they are in stasis, meaning that they, obviously, are neither alive nor dead."

"Yeah, yeah. I see. So the soul, the spirit? It's still there, then?" she asked.

"Oh," Hadley suddenly took on a more solemn, more ceremonial air. "Well that. We assure our clients, and their families that indeed, that the soul is, in our opinion, still with the body."

"Does...does a body, a patient, know what's going on around them?"

"No, absolutely not. The body, as well as the mind, is in stasis. Therefore there is no brainwave activity, because all functions are arrested, and perfectly preserved. So there is no undue mental distress. Dreaming, or any other awareness of outside stimulus.

"You must understand, Miss Wheatley, cryopreservation is death forestalled. Keep in mind, resuscitation can be performed minutes, even hours at a time after one been legally declared dead. So death, in the legal sense, is when all options towards reviving a patient have been absolutely exhausted."

"Fascinating!" she said. "So, do you got a sperm bank in here?"

"Huh?!" Hadley was startled at the sudden shift in subject. "Oh, um, I'm afraid we aren't as yet, equipped for—!"

"Thank the lord for small favors!" Ora shouted, as though at Sunday services.

"I'm sorry, I don't. . ."

Ora leveled another hard, heavy gaze. "Why don't you tell people that HaloGen is a subsidiary of CryoGen? I'm sure if people knew they'd be real uptight about having bodies, NOT PATIENTS, so close to their food.

"'Scuse, me, not close. . . *are*. Are their food. Did you even think about what you were doing to people? Children getting sick off—"

"Miss Wheatley! Your accusation are unfounded and simply outrageous!" Hadley's face ran flush with anger. "I'll have to ask you to leave now."

"I had to come here to see it for myself. Providence in action." Ora rose to leave.

"If you've tampered with anything in this facility—!"

"Oh, chile. You've got nothing to worry about from me. It's them down there! They're not just frozen, doc. They're trapped. Bound. And they know. *They know.*"

"Get out, before I call the police!"

Hadley watched as Ora left his office, and in the silence, everything came rushing at him: How a late shipment of liquid nitrogen resulted in patient thawing...

He remembered when he and his team inspected the bodies, they found rodents had somehow gotten into the tanks, and had gotten fat from taking almost their fill. They noticed other, more startling, things as well.

The tanks held four people at a time. Miraculously, there were eight forms. Four bodies. Four replicas. The replicas being *ghosts*. The rats seemed to enjoy the ghosts more than they did the actual bodies. And Hadley could understand why. The aroma that breathed off of the frozen, ethereal beings was intoxicating. It only seemed natural to want to eat it. And when he finally did, the experience for him was transcendent. As though he had truly ingested the flesh of divinity. Of manna from heaven!

Hadley went out the side door from his office, which led to the ice cream vats. The sweet scent of the *Brozia* caught his nose. When he got to the landing of the bottom stair, he noticed that the door to one of the machines was ajar, and that there was a froth of *Brozia* spilling down the side and onto the floor.

"Fuckin' bitch!"

He went over to the machine, and made an awful discovery: The *Brozia* looked darker, somehow, and smelled faintly of. . .

"How? Oh, shitshitshit. . ."

John Dimes

. . . chocolate.

Brozia didn't respond well to the presence of chocolate. Something inherent in its chemical properties broke down the cellular inhibiting agent infused in its mix. It took a terrible exhibition of some eight screaming laboratory rats to prove that fact some time ago.

Hadley shook as all the machines on the factory floor began rocking, and bubbling forth dark matter, until various jellied shapes coalesced into the forms of men and women. Some roved independently. Others were fused together in shambling Man-O-War-like colonies of anguished ghosts. Muddy hands slapped him, and ground into Hadley's face. Quietly they touched his lips, and forced themselves into mouth. . .smothering him in an endless tide of themselves. . .

-SOH-

Outside, Ora found Zan sitting alone at the foot of the stairs.

"How long you been sitting here, baby?"

"I don't know," Zan said, staring up at her

queasily. "I. . . I think I threw up again, though."

"Poor baby." She gave him a tender peck on the forehead. "I bet you did."

Gently, she wiped the chocolate stains from his mouth with her sleeve.

Room 409
Joseph McGee

The voices echoed through the paper-thin walls.

The world inside room 409 was much different from the life Michael Richardson had known before the explosion of verbal gunfire with his soon-to-be ex-wife. It was his idea to stay at the Inn until things had calmed down enough to gather his belongings, and finally vacate his house.

It was his grandfather's stories that had attracted him to the Inn, though he had never stayed there before tonight. He had always wondered in the back of his mind what really was there.

Ending his eight years of marriage didn't worry him much. It had been a long, drawn out battle of words, and neither of them could stand it for another moment. It was for the best, he consoled himself.

Voices filtered from down the hall of the fourth floor, whispering someone else's memories of forgotten history at the Winter Moon Inn, just off of I-95.

It was a cozy brick building with an adobe roof, a beautifully carpeted interior in the foyer and friendly and hospitable staff.

Michael knew that no one else would ever rent one of the rooms on the fourth floor, so he requested the most peaceful room in the building. "I-want-room-four-oh-nine," he demanded the clerk in the lobby, refusing to listen to any objections that he might have, to get the hotel manager.

The clerk consulted with his boss, who was reluctant to let him have the electronic key, but a whispered argument won the battle for Michael Richardson.

The manager gave him the key with a sorrowful look on his face as if to say *buddy, you don't know what you're getting yourself into.* The words had become a mantra that he repeated silently to any and all guests that requested rooms on the fourth floor; fortunately there weren't too many that did.

But Michael did.

He wasn't certain that the stories he had been told decades ago were true, but the hesitation to allow him to have room 409 proved right that something had happened there a long time ago, and may still be happening to this day. One way or another, Michael needed a place to stay for a few days while the dust settled from the blowout between husband and wife, and if not for Grandpa Jensen, room 409 at the Winter Moon Inn would've never existed to him.

His grandfather once told him it was just like that *Jack Nicholson* flick, *The Shining*. He just hoped that a naked dead woman wouldn't emerge from the bathtub and choke him.

Grandpa Jensen would normally say such stories were poppycock. That was his word to describe bogus things. Even when he would joke, and have that mean, stern face he would sometimes crack and say poppycock.

That night, the grey haze of the crescent moon hung over a clear sky snuck through the slits in the blinds; the only other light that protruded the room was that of a neon alarm clock that he was allowed to take from his house to wake up in the morning to go to his nine-to-five at Peterson's Technology Center, where he was a data processor.

143

Michael had taken the next two weeks of from work to deal with his marital crisis.

He sat on the full bed of his hotel room and stared out the glass sliding door of the balcony, watching the winter sun change the sky from a dirty grey to a bright red-orange.

He had hoped to see her—but the Woman in White showed her face very seldom, his grandfather had said. And when Grandpa Jensen told him what the police had said about her suicide, he said it was poppycock. He had known back then, like Michael knew now, that her death was no accident, no suicide—but murder.

And he could still see his grandpa standing there, with his white as snow hair, and wrinkled skin, talking about the hotel that had been so famous for its extravagant guest list back in the day. Even public officials had rested their heads on the pillows of the Winter Moon Inn.

It had been known for hosting some of Hollywood's most honorable celebrities—as well death and horror that the local papers seem to fixate on back in the early fifties.

Joseph McGee

-SOH-

The following night, Michael laid his head on his plush pillow beneath the three layers of blankets, and he couldn't help but think of what his wife was doing now. The best thing he could do to end his feelings for her, he figured, was to think of her fucking another man. Jumping his bones right now; screaming into the wind like thunder in the sky; shaking, clawing, and grabbing at one another.

He stayed wide awake, alone.

He checked the clock on the night stand. 4:12, it read.

He heard the voices again, this time louder and concrete, as if someone was at his bedside all along, watching his slumber before finally attacking the unsuspecting soul He scrambled out of his bed, allowing his eyes to adjust to the night—and then he saw her. It was the woman in the white wedding gown. Rumors that floated around claimed that she was killed hours before her wedding by someone that stayed or worked at this hotel.

He stood there, still, frozen with fear. He couldn't utter anything more than a soft grumble of nothing. He felt faint, dizzy; adrenaline pumping in, surging through his veins, gave him the urge to find the quickest escape from his room. Or yell. Yell as loud as his voice could carry. Someone on the next floor would surely hear him, and call the lobby to complain about the noise. Some *had* to.

She looked at him, her body transparent in the darkness; her face was ghostly, her jaw strained and her eyes hollow; she floated as if weightless from the air.

The apparition had a trance over him; she somehow calmed him in the darkness of the night. He walked towards here, zombie-likc. His eyes went blank, in and out of a coherent state of mind.

She seduced him. She lathered her decaying tongue on his face, but all he saw was a beautiful twenty-something woman.

She had made him fall back into the bed, arms apart as she unfastened his belt. "Do you want me?" she asked faintly.

"I love you," Michael uncontrollably said.

She lifted the bottom of her dress off, peeling off her panties and planted her hips on his waist. It felt real. Warm. Tight. Throbbing. Like there was no place else he'd rather be than at room 409 with his ghost-lover. He grew inside of her as she slowly lifted herself and slammed down on him, faster with each thrust. And when he could hold himself back no longer, as she buckled, he released himself into her, partially staining her gown.

He didn't cry out or moan. Michael was lying as if he was in a vegetable state, though his erection was proof that his body still functioned; still hard afterward, and he could've easily gone another round. But the woman in white got off of him. As he came to, out of his trance attempting to understand what had just happened, he could not remember a single thought, as if a chunk of his memory was simply cut from time.

Her face grew mean, her brow pushed down and her lips tightened, and with a deep growl, she said "You cheated on me! How could you," and she began to cry in a raspy demonic tone.

Michael lifted himself from the bed, heart pounding, pants puddled around his ankles, and he looked down at himself, stiff. His eyes widened. "Who the hell— What the hell are you?"

She never gave a response. She again climbed on

top of him.

He was paralyzed, not from fear, but from *something* else.

Her transparent arms plunged deep into his chest. She twitched and wiggled, clawed and ripped, and tore his flesh open with a spray of blood painting the walls.

She pulled it out of him.

And in his dying seconds, he saw his own heart beating one last time in her hands, before she vanished into the night of room 409.

Grave Robber

Benjamin Bussey

My shoulders are like lead. The battered work shirt sticks cold and wet to my back, and I taste dirt in my mouth and throat with every breath. I've been dragging cartfuls of bricks all day - the latest of many short term jobs - and every burning muscle in my body is telling me to plant myself down in the first bar I come across and flush out all that dust in my gullet with as many beers as my lousy paycheck can buy. Every ache in my back, every blister on my hands and feet is telling me not to think about tomorrow or where the hell the next paycheck's gonna come from and just drown it all away, flood my contracted guts and wash all those other thoughts away with it.

But now I'm at the bar with my first beer in my hand already half drained, and all of a sudden I'm looking into the eyes of a fallen angel with jet black hair and ivory skin, and she's looking right back.

Grave Robber

This is one of those times when you really do have to ask what a girl like that is doing in a place like this. She's way too high class for this dump. Fur coat down to her slender ankles, long black cigarette holder on the end of some exotic brand I can't pronounce; the whole package. But seeing as she is in a place like this, and she's eye to eye with a two-bit bum like me, it can only mean one thing. And I pray to God that that one thing is what I hope it is.

She smiles and it's as if somebody just put the lights on. She says her name is Ariana, Ariana Delaney, and the words drip from her mouth like honey. I bullshit, and when she laughs I get a whiff of her breath, so sweet it almost makes me not notice how bad I stink. I'm waiting for the ground to fall from under me with every passing second but somehow I can't put a foot wrong with this dame. Every sleazy line comes off like a sonnet; every sly glance down to check out the goods is welcomed. Before I even stop to think about it, every muscle in my body has forgotten its exhaustion and is screaming at me to get a little more exercise, some of the better kind.

When she asks me to come back to her place, I

can't say yes fast enough.

-SOH-

The limo's rocking every yard of the drive back. It's a pretty sweet ride, quality leather interior, but I'm way too preoccupied with this angel to care. We're there before I know it. I take all of a nanosecond to admire the plush mansion before I'm collapsed on her four poster and she's riding me like a bronco, shoving me headfirst into an express elevator to heaven and crying my bum name like it was the name of God. Every bead of sweat that falls from her forehead is a taste from the fountain of eternal youth. Our bodies are burning together from the waist out, and I don't wanna stop until we're nothing but ash and smoke. I keep looking in her eyes and there's a hunger there like I've never seen, the kind that can never be satisfied, the kind that eats people whole, and I've never wanted more to be eaten alive, every last ounce of flesh consumed by this incredible animal woman.

A couple of minutes later and she tells me she has to take a shower. Doesn't say a word about me needing one. Like I thought, she's the kind that likes the grease. The bedroom adjoins to a bathroom about as big as my apartment and she leaves the door wide open, the light and steam pouring out in swirls, floating more of that sweet smell towards the bed where I lie still trying to catch my breath. My focus slips and I'm a blink away from sleep when something catches my eye. There's a glint from the dresser by the door. Something damn shiny and damn big. Just that bit shiny and big enough to get me up and out of bed.

It's a diamond the size of a tangerine. In the shadow of many colorful bottles of expensive looking perfumes and oils, with the light and steam from the bathroom billowing around it, it's like a goddamned stained glass window. It's beautiful, almost enough to put its owner to shame. I can only imagine what it's worth, and imagine I do, I imagine all sorts of shit, like grabbing it and getting the fuck out of there before her ladyship gets out of the shower. Then the desire strikes to see what that gorgeous body of hers looks like wet and I stay put, kidding myself I'm being decent by not ripping her off then and there.

A shadow falls in the doorway, and all of a

sudden I'm eye to eye with the fallen angel again. I'm so distracted by this rock I didn't even hear the water stop running. She's leaning against the doorframe with a glint in her eye, light spilling over her shoulders, and there's a white towel around her waist, leaving that magnificent torso bare and glistening with moisture. This was definitely a sight worth sticking around to see.

You noticed my little family heirloom she says, voice soft as marshmallow.

I'd hardly call that little I reply, trying my damnedest not to sound dumbstruck.

She picks it by its ornate silver chain and pops it over her neck. With that big beautiful sucker hanging down that cleavage, it's a struggle to decide what to keep my eyes on.

Pretty, ain't it she purrs, like the cat that got the cream and wouldn't mind a refill.

I'm probably drooling and I don't care if she notices. I tell her I can see the hunger in her eyes, but can't for the life of me figure out what a woman like her could be going hungry for.

Oh really she says, that kitten voice a little wounded.

153

Grave Robber

I tell her she's got it all, looks and money. She's what every man wants and every woman wants to be.

She looks at me for a second, a look I can't quite read. She turns, yanks the towel loose and rubs herself down, then drops the towel on the tiled bathroom floor and walks around me to the other side of the dresser where she gets one of her exotic cigarettes. She lights it up and the pale smoke dances around her firm white body in the steamy light, naked except for the diamond.

So you think I'm the woman who has everything she sighs, handing me her lit cigarette and lighting herself another. Next to my usual brand, it tastes like steak and potatoes.

I tell her I can't believe what I'm looking at, and I mean it. That body, that face - that diamond. You are that diamond, and that diamond is you, I tell her.

This old thing? She laughs, like a baby. *This is nothing. This is leftovers. You should see the real Delaney jewels.*

I try to keep my eyes from getting any wider.

My goddamn grandmother she hisses. Curses sound like poetry from her lips. *She was the one who had all the real good stuff. Rubies. Emeralds. Plenty*

154

more diamonds, this size and bigger. Rings, necklaces and brooches of gold, silver and platinum. An honest to God Aladdin's Cave. And I didn't get a goddamn thing but this.

What do you mean? I ask. I gotta try to sound less interested.

She laughs that baby laugh again and it stabs me in the heart. *You wouldn't believe me if I told you* she says.

I'm really struggling not to look interested now. Try me, I say.

She takes a long, lingering drag on her cigarette, sucks the smoke back and savors the grade 'A' flavor, and lets it pour out through her nostrils. My aching body's waking up again.

The old lady got buried with it she says. *All according to her will. The rings stayed on her dead fingers, the brooches on her dead wrists, necklaces round her dead neck; even a goddamned diamond tiara on her cold dead noggin. Aladdin's Cave was buried with her down at old Browning's Cemetery. Old hag makes Scrooge look like Robin Hood.*

Those tiny white bare feet take a step in my direction.

Grave Robber

Bet you would have loved to see it all she murmurs. *You think this rock is something? You haven't seen anything.*

What's a horde of treasure like that worth? I say, stepping toward her and putting my filthy hand around her soft clean hip.

Wouldn't you like to know she smiles, her bare waist rubbing up to mine.

Couple of million? I venture, pulling her hard against me.

If not more she whispers, her leg wrapping around mine.

The next twenty minutes or so are a blur of sweat and thrusting. She falls asleep right after, and my aching body that hasn't seen sleep in almost twenty-four hours is telling me what to do again.

Couple of million. *If not more.*

My burning muscles find strength again. She's asleep for sure now and I can't get out of the door fast enough.

-SOH-

One quick visit to the handyman's work shed

156

later and I'm out on my way to Browning's Cemetery with a shovel and a flashlight. Greed has cooled my blood. I'm not as lovedrunk as I was on arrival so I've got my bearings a lot better now. I know where I am, and I know that Browning's is only about a mile east of here. I can handle that on foot. My only alternative would be to check out Ms. Delaney's indubitably large and lavish car collection and take my pick, but with the size of the robbery I'm about to make it seems only smart to avoid getting any excess heat on my shoulders. No need to go crazy here. Plenty of time for that once I've made my score. My course of action is simple. I dig up the grave, grab the loot, and fill the grave back in. If things go smoothly, nobody will ever even know about it. People spend a lifetime looking for an opportunity like this and it's fallen right in my lap. I'm past the cemetery gates in no time. The night is black, humid and silent as the grave, except for my heart, pumping adrenaline into my veins like gasoline on a flame. Can't let it dizzy me. Can't afford to lose my focus, not now.

I hadn't reckoned on how damned big the cemetery is. I'm squatting as I hop from grave to grave, flashlight beam washing over every headstone, looking for that one name, the name that spells my future –

Dorothy Jean Delaney. There it is in bold, deep-chiseled lettering. Glancing around, I notice that all the surrounding graves belong to those formerly of the Delaney clan. They're probably worth a look too, on the chance that the rest of the family were as possessive of their earthly goods. But only after I'm done with Granny. Tossing aside the flashlight and sucking the damp night air hard into my chest, I thrust the shovel into the earth and throw the dirt aside. I dig in again, arms and back weary from a day of hard labor and a night of hard passion. I dig in again, the blood in my arms heavy and hot. I dig in again, feeling every vein throb, reminding myself I'm only six feet away from Aladdin's Cave.

It feels like a half a lifetime has passed when I thrust the shovel into the loose soil once more and finally hit something hard, but instead of that dull thud you expect when hitting wood I hear a shrill clank. I've hit metal. Jesus, this is one wacky family.

Getting down to my knees, my sweat-drenched hands brush away the last of the dirt and find the edges of the iron coffin lid. This is it. Payday; maybe the last one I'll ever need. I get back on my feet, ram the shovel into the join, and heave. Not a budge. I heave harder, harder, and I'm burning again, but this time it's a fire I want out of right now; I want into this goddamned coffin if it's the last thing I do on this earth.

I heave - and at last the lid comes loose. There's a gust of stale air and a noise like the last dying breath of a punctured tire. Even what's left on me of Ariana's sweet smell can't disguise what's on the air now; it's the stink of death, and there's no escaping it. But I don't want to escape it. Not right now.

-SOH-

I open the coffin to see my future.

There's nothing there.

It's a black hole. There's no body. There's no bottom to the coffin. There's just a black empty space, an abyss – with a small wooden staircase leading straight down. This is no coffin. It's a door. That's what Ariana meant by Aladdin's Cave. She wasn't speaking allegorically. She meant it's a real goddamn cave. This night sure couldn't get much weirder.

My nerves are dancing, but I shake them off. Sure, I don't have the first clue what's down there, but I'm not the type of guy to set out on a marathon only to give it up at the last mile. I haven't hit the wall yet and I'm not about to. Crossing my fingers that the wooden steps can take my weight, I head on down, my heart in my throat.

The stench of death is so bad down here I can taste it. I gag and try to breathe only through my mouth even though it doesn't make a shit bit of difference. It was dark outside but it's even darker down here, as black as Ariana's hair, and I don't know what's waiting for me as my foot leaves the last step of the wooden staircase with a creak that's straight out of a carnival spook house. My foot lands on what feels like solid enough ground, but I can't see it to be sure. Damn it, I left the flashlight on the surface. Do I turn back? To hell with it. I've got a lighter and that'll have to do. I flick it open and rub my thumb down the coarse metal. Foom. Let there be light.

Jesus. I almost wish I'd stayed in the dark. It's like what I'd imagine the inside of a pig's ass looks like. I'm surrounded by walls of mud, all sticky and oily, with roots sticking out here and there, and that rotten death stink is even thicker. There's a tunnel ahead of me, six high by four wide at most. Damn, it's tight, and when I look down it I can't see the end. Never thought of myself as claustrophobic, but now I'm here. I start taking steps forward in the dim light of the flickering flame, breaking my way through sheets of cobweb. Damn. Never thought I was arachnophobic either. Christ, this really is a spook house.

I'm walking. Still no end in sight to the tunnel. I try not to worry about it. I feel something brush over my leg. I don't look down. I keep walking. This is nothing. Just a stinking hole in the ground. Nothing to be scared of. Not when the treasure trove awaits.

But now there's a weird, high-pitched scurrying sound. I keep looking dead ahead, and anytime a word like *'trapped'* or *'buried alive'* comes into my head I try to replace it with a mantra of *'diamonds, gold, platinum, rubies.'* But it's not working. That weird screech keeps coming and things are crawling around my feet and even though I don't want to know what it is, it's getting harder and harder not to look.

I look down. Suddenly I remember Dwight Frye in the old Dracula movie.

Rats. Rats. Thousands. Millions of them.

Never thought I was rodent-phobic. But here I am. And there they are. Sweet fucking Christ. Big fat hairy bodies wriggling and scratching over every inch of floor as far as the eye can see. For a moment I can't move. I don't know where to go, what to do, anything. I can't go back now. I can't. Diamonds. Rubies. Silver, gold, platinum.

I run. I run as fast as I can without hitting the walls, trying not to trip when my feet land on the big furry bastards. I realize they're running toward me. Good. If they're not going the same way I'm going then hopefully there won't be any of them there when I reach the treasure. The diamonds, the emeralds, the gold; it's all here for the taking. I just have to get there. The tunnel stretches out like the highway at night. There's no end in sight but I can never see more than a few feet ahead of me so it could be any time now, any time.

The ground disappears beneath my feet. Fuck. I'm falling.

I drop about six feet before I hit the ground face-first. The wind's knocked out of me but I'm okay. It'll take more than that to finish me off. Time to get up and see where I am now.

-SOH-

That burning sensation in my muscles is back with full force as I wheeze my way up onto my feet and I realize how dog-tired I really am. Ignore it. Ignore it just a little while longer. This has to be it. But I dropped my lighter when I fell and the flame's gone out, so once again I can't see shit. I'm almost afraid to drop back down to my knees and start pawing to find it in case there are more rats or I don't want to think what else lurking nearby. But without the lighter I'm completely blind, and I don't want to be blind down here, especially as the stink of death is even worse down here than it was before. It's so warm and damp and the smell is so rank it's like being inside a hollowed out pumpkin leftover from Halloween, rotting in the sun on somebody's front step, except there's no sun, and no moon either. There's absolutely no light anywhere and I can't take it anymore.

I find the lighter. I spark it to life.

Suddenly everything's shiny.

This is it.

There's treasure everywhere. The chamber is a good ten high by twenty wide and there's even more down here than Ariana said there was. Big-ass statues and trinkets of gold and silver. Strings of pearls. Puddles of precious stones. Heaps of gold coins straight out of a pirate story. We're talking tens, maybe even hundreds of millions here. And there at the center of it all on a cold stone slab is Granny, flat on her back, still, dank, dead. Forget Aladdin's Cave; it's a Pharaoh's tomb. True to Ariana's word, Granny's dressed in all her finest – rings, brooches, necklaces, and yes, even a diamond tiara. Amazing the weight of them hasn't crushed her bones to powder yet. Then a shiver goes up my spine as I notice how well preserved the corpse is. She barely even looks like she's decomposing yet. That can't be right. I didn't catch the date on the tombstone but the grave didn't look like it was filled in too recently, and Ariana sure wasn't talking like she'd only just lost the old lady. But none of this is important. The treasure is mine, all within arm's reach. All I have to do is reach out and take it.

There's a diamond around Granny's neck. Sure enough, it's even bigger and more beautiful than Ariana's, even if it doesn't look nearly as good against this sagging weathered carcass as Ariana's did against her perfect breasts. It was that diamond that drew me here, so it seems only fitting, poetic even, that Granny's diamond be the first thing I take. I reach down to pick the big rock up, brushing Granny's dead skin. Weird. She's not even that cold. My gut clenches and I know something is seriously not right. Ignore it. Ignore it, goddamn it. You're a rich man now.

I grab the rock and in the same instant Granny's eyes flash open.

I come within a hair's breadth of pissing myself.

I drop the rock and back off. Granny's eyes don't close. Granny looks right at me, eyes all wide and smiling, and she starts to get up. I back off further.

And there I was thinking this night had already gotten as weird as it could.

Granny's on her feet now and she sure isn't acting like someone who should be dead. Her mouth hangs open and this weird and horrible hissing noise comes out. She's reaching out for me, her blunt brown teeth are bared, and she sounds like a pissed off rattlesnake. I want to hit her with something but I left the shovel up on the ground and somehow I don't think it's a good idea to get close enough to punch this thing. She might do something unexpected, like grab my arm and rip it out at the socket. I want to turn and try to figure if I can get out of here the way I fell in, but I don't think it'd be a good idea to turn my back on her either.

She keeps on making that rattlesnake hiss and suddenly there's another noise, the sound of big stones moving. It's hard to make out by the tiny flame of my lighter, particularly as I don't wanna take my eyes off Granny, but it seems that the walls at the back of the chamber are sliding apart, opening the chamber up. A sickness comes in the pit of my stomach as I realize what that means.

The entire Delaney clan is buried alongside Granny.

Guess who's coming to dinner.

Next thing I know there's a good twenty or thirty old dead people closing in on me, all gray-blue skinned and bug-eyed, mouths wide open and hands stretching out, each one hissing like Granny, the sound coming at me like one giant hiss from some gigantic fucking king cobra. My back's to the wall, and I know there's no escape but I reach up to find the ledge I fell down from anyway, and before I know it there are fingernails ripping into the skin of my arm and teeth biting through cartilage and muscle. Pain shoots through my body, and with it comes panic. I scream like a girl at the sight of my own blood squirting out, all red and dark and smelling like rusty metal, and I can't help but fall cowering into the corner. I'm easy pickings now. The teeth and nails are sinking into me all over, gnawing at my ankles, heaving up my kneecaps, digging into my thighs, bursting my balls, slicing my dick, ripping out my intestines, cracking open my ribcage, pulling out my heart, puncturing my windpipe, tugging out my tongue, tearing open my cheeks and piercing my eyeballs.

Just as the taste of my own blood and vomit floods my nose, the pain takes over and the lights go out completely, the damnedest thing happens. In my head, I see Ariana's smiling white face. It's in close-up, but fractured, as if I'm seeing it reflected in a mirror ball, or through the eyes of a fly or something. And I realize that she's looking at me through the diamond, it's like her goddamned crystal ball and she's using it to watch me die, and she's smiling while I'm eaten alive by however many of her dearly departed relatives.

Guess I've got time for one final thought. That's the last time I accept an offer to go home with a glamorous stranger, no matter how high class she is. Rich broads. You just can't trust them.

ROCK & ROLL IS DEAD
Eric Enck

If "Cowboy" Sam Hutton was alive today, he might cherish the memories that kept him in Delaware. The beaches, the nightclubs in the summer—even the distant and low feeling, like being poisoned every time he clocked in and clocked out.

The building where Sam Hutton worked housed 15.7 (the area's up and coming radio station), and its old walls needed a paint job.

The station dealt classic and hard rock. Classic rock during the day and hard rock at night. After all, nights belonged to harder edges—young couples drifting with summer winds, winding down roads and finding slippery kisses lost in the dark.

15.7 FM had been in existence for only a few months after the licensing agreement with the station, along with FCC regulations, helped the owner find a suitable business arrangement.

The station was small and subtle, located in

Slaughter Beach, Delaware. During the day automatic machines ran it. Rerun shows of DJ's from the station's previous incarnations.

The owner's two sons trained Sam. Max and Jason Waters, who were both very tall and similar looking young men but polar opposites of each other. They showed him how to do everything his job entailed and asked him for his bank account information for direct deposit of his paychecks. That was the last time he saw anyone there again.

Sam walked to the old brick building, which was his nightly task. His broadcasting room was no bigger than a boiler room, where between requests the midnight wind would blow through the hollows in the building.

Sam didn't think he had a good radio voice but the owner didn't seem to mind, and if she did she never said anything. He had yet to meet her. He only knew her name was Kara Waters. Her sons had not spoken of her in high esteem, saying only that she was very wealthy and didn't come around much.

There wasn't another building or facility for miles. Just Sam Hutton, his microphone, tapes and equipment tucked in the radio station under a starry

170

sky. Sitting in the low-lit room, "Cowboy" discovered how lonely a person could feel in a new environment.

Donning the microphone that first night, he introduced himself as "Cowboy."

He learned from a few callers 15.7 THE BEACH was the only rock station in the area and they appreciated having some good music to cruise the nights to. Alone on the airwaves and frightened by the building itself, he was grateful his callers didn't know of his fear. In the radio station, he had a tremendous sense he was being watched.

On his third shift when he clocked in, he took a seat by his booth as thunderstorms raged outside. He took his first caller but not before feeling the pulse in his temple quicken. Sam started wondering just how the hell he got this job without talking to the boss first.

Maybe she's one of those rich women that just don't have time to talk to lowly DJ's like you Sam...

"This is WGH 15.7 FM THE BEACH—the greatest rock and roll station in the world—who is this?"

"Hey guy!"

"Hey hey hey, would you like to request a song?"

"Boy, would I," the voice said. "How 'bout

Welcome Home by *Sphinx?*"

"Sphinx?" Sam asked. "Are they local?"

"Sure are, Cowboy," the voice said. "They used to be the best local band in the area. Lead singer killed himself...*hung himself.*"

Cowboy looked around the room. He heard thunder crash outside and pictured the lightning stretching across the sky in jagged lines of violet violence.

"He..." Cowboy said.

"Hung himself." The voice repeated. "Had his feet dipped in motor oil, too. Cops couldn't figure out why at first, but it was in case he changed his mind—slip off the chair anyway."

Cowboy responded with silence.

"God, they were good though. The *greatest.*"

"What song would you like to hear from them again?" Cowboy asked.

"I like *Welcome Home.* But if you can't find it, how about *Down Here with Us?* It was a great song; Layne Wolf could really howl man."

"Layne...Wo..."

"Wolf," the voice finished for him. "Layne Wolf, lead singer. Hey, while you're working tonight

Cowboy, my wife wanted to know if you'd tell a few more of those jokes like you do."

"Oh sure," Cowboy said. "I'm always doing that. I'll tell you what Mr...."

"George."

"George, I'll get *Sphinx* on for you, okay my man? Thanks for scaring the hell out of me by the way."

George laughed. "Hey, no problem buddy!"

Hanging the phone up, Sam looked at its coiled wire and thought of a man he'd never seen before, hanging himself with his pants rolled up and his legs slick with 10-W-30 motor oil. Standing there on a chair waiting for the right moment to take a short walk into darkness.

Stop it! You've been here three whole days and you're already freaked out about this place.

But the cold...and there was only one window, only one door (two if you counted that closet with a toilet in it). The ON AIR sign sometimes went out from faulty electricity. The sensation that getting a job this cool was, was just, well...too *damn* easy was something Cowboy couldn't shake. And there was a steady, slow water drip that fell in between his compulsions to scream.

Layne Wolf, he slipped.

Cowboy pushed away from the table and computers. Then he searched the libraries of programs and found *Sphinx,* but just before the computer screen went dead. The lights went out. He thought maybe he pulled the cord from the wall after moving so quickly, distracted by his thoughts. He saw his own eyes, glowing in the reflection of the computer monitor, red and bright. Sam threw off his headphones, got to his feet, turned and screamed. The ON AIR sign said something else.

Something impossible.

NO LIFE, flashed at him.

Cowboy paced back and forth for a few moments—the booming thunder made his heart race—and then the computer came back on, the lights hummed and flickered and everything was up and running again. He could feel the hollow cool of dampness throughout the station. It reminded him of basements. The air felt oppressive and chilly, almost like silk. The kind that lined coffins—the kind of coffins where things began to open their eyes and unfold their arms in Sam's mind.

Just get through this night, that's all...

Time hung like a dead man. Each day he clocked in but felt he would never clock out. There was something wrong about this radio station, and it wasn't just the fact that the call numbers 15.7 added up to thirteen.

-SOH-

For the next few days a scattered sequence of murders went unnoticed.

-SOH-

Delaware came alive like a virus caught in a bloodstream. "Cowboy" caught the attention of all the rock and roll fans in the First State. Even Wesson Daxter, who up until yesterday had kept from killing his neighbor, got caught up in the "Cowboy" frenzy. Wesson called into the station and requested a song by *Led Zeppelin*. He then dropped what he was doing by the kitchen sink, picked up a large crescent wrench and walked across Broad Kill Street with the gift of moonlight shining in his stare, silver and maddening.

The old woman was sitting on her porch smoking a cigarette. The police would find her laying with legs spread, arms out to the side, clutching the windowsill while her brains dried on the leaves of her hanging spider plants. Wesson had beaten her to death while humming the song he requested, until whatever thoughts the old woman had been thinking were running down her misshapen face.

Her porch needed painting anyway, Wesson laughed while he stood there with blood all over his face. The low summer wind that carried leaves in a dance of misery taunted him. Walking back to his house he smiled a shark-like grin, went upstairs and cut his wrists with a bottle opener. He wrote his name on the wall in his blood, but not before calling into 15.7 FM THE BEACH and requesting another song.

The State Police would be busy for awhile figuring out why a preacher would do such a thing.

-SOH-

Cowboy was discovering horrible truths about

the place he worked at. Like whispers he could sometimes hear in his headphones above the songs. Or the walls that seemed to grow.

In the closet-sized bathroom, there was the ghost he'd found when he had gone to take a long back-stretching leak. That's when he'd noticed the girl in the corner by the sink, watching him.

The girl's shoulders were cold under her moth-eaten silk dress. She started to sing while Cowboy screamed. When she opened her mouth, Cowboy saw the hole through the back of her head where the gun had done its job. The skilled hands of a pathologist had removed her brains and wads of cotton hung there instead.

It keeps the face from sinking in at the viewings...you know that, Cowboy? You came all the way from New Hampshire to find that out

-SOH-

A group of teenagers vacationing from Pennsylvania, staying at a beach motel, called into the "Cowboy" and requested a heavy metal song by a band named *Crypt.* As the song played through the

177

teenager's speakers they attacked each other viciously. The three men beat their girlfriends to death.

-SOH-

Every night he'd sit in that booth, turn the switch that lit up the sign that said ON AIR, and think of how he'd be responsible for several murders and unexplained deaths in Delaware.

Not he...

It...

ON AIR

NO LIFE

Cowboy had been a D.J. in *New York* once, but never dealt with anything like this.

-SOH-

Beth Eaby and her young daughter were indoors during the hot summer day as crickets sang a forgotten tune outside. As Beth finished doing the dishes she turned her kitchen radio to 15.7 FM. Classic rock during the day, modern rock at night.

Both different but both *very* delicious.

She picked up her phone to request a song.

Beth was waiting for her husband Carl, when she looked out into her living room and saw the *My Pal* doll she hated her daughter playing with.

"Hello? Hello, this is the Cowboy! You got a song request?"

"Yes," Beth said. "I'd like to hear something from *KISS*—anything."

"You got it," Cowboy said. "What's your name, babe?"

"Beth."

"Beth!" Cowboy laughed. "Sure thing, baby doll, and how about we play two songs for you tonight?"

"Okay." Beth said. "Thank you."

"No problem. Who's your number one station in Delaware, Beth?"

"One-Five-Seven, THE BEACH!" Beth laughed.

She hung up the phone, and in minutes she heard the song come on the radio. It was *her* song; the one *she* requested. The band *she* requested. The station had just finished with Aerosmith as the garbage disposal did its job eating the remains of tonight's dinner.

The song was *Beth* by *KISS,* although she no longer knew it after the first few lines from Peter Chris' raspy vocals.

She was in her own mind, walking...

That was when I hit the little bitch. I hit her hard—square on the bridge of the nose with a hammer—and watched in delight as her funny, laughing face caved in and gushed red-black blood.

I smiled, knowing that I had finally killed her.

And that was when she started laughing at me, her wicked pink plastic face melding back together from the blow I'd dealt her. I let out a deep sigh and reached for the hacksaw amidst the pile of torture implements scattered on the table.

I bought her for my daughter's fourth birthday.

I remember walking into the toy section of Wal-Mart, sweating under those phosphorescent lights as I turned a corner and faced a thousand My Pal dolls, smiling defiantly from the windows of their bright pink boxes. Out of the corner of my eye, I saw them turn their tiny heads and grin at me, showing little pairs of fangs as I walked past them. I hate them!

Ever since I was a kid, I was aware of the truth about dolls.

Eric Enck

I was five and my parents had let me stay up late to watch Fantasy Island on TV. You know, the one with the midget named "Tattoo"? And in that episode, I realized dolls come to life at midnight and run amok.

I took the hacksaw in my hand and pondered over the doll bound in the tiny red plastic chair, where she had been drinking tea next to the teddy bear before my daughter went to bed.

Dolls!

Forget what you think you know about dolls.

Never mind that bear, he's okay in my book and he doesn't say much. But dolls...

They sleep during the day and wake up when everyone is in bed. Plastic ones, porcelain (those are the worst!), cloth, wood or whatever, the whole lots of them come to life at night like the little vampires they really are.

Forget the hacksaw!

They walk around houses and streets at night doing god knows what! I think they even have their own social system.

I'll plug in my husband's skill-saw, open the throttle full bore and point the blade at Pal's face as I grin over her.

"Now you're really gonna get it!"

I swear it! Remember when you were a little kid and you used to talk to your toys? They'd answer you back, wouldn't they? Don't tell me that they didn't because you and I both know that they did!

Gosh this song's good!

I put the saw up to Pal's neck and she starts to scream as the blade rips through her throat. Bright red blood and pink plastic sawdust sprays the room. I grin as Pal's head falls off the bloody pink stump of her neck onto the floor. I give her head a strong kick for good measure and watch it streak across the playroom and bounce off the wall.

"Take that, Pal!" I laugh. Downstairs, I go to grab a cold one after a hard day's work. I slump in my chair and click on the tube to wait for my husband, but quickly change it to In Search Of... hosted by Spock from Star Trek when a "Talking Tina" commercial comes on. I can still hear my song playing on the radio—what the hell? The front door opens and there I see my husband drop his bags. I don't know why Carl would—

Carl did drop his bags. He stared at his wife. She was covered in blood, but not from something that terrified her as a child.

"What's wrong, honey?" she asked.

"What happened to you?"

"Whatever do you mean?"

"Your face, your hair. Jesus, Beth. Were you in an accident?"

And then Carl saw it, looking past the shoulders of his wife, who had that lost look in her eyes as a KISS song playing loudly spilled out from the kitchen. *Two Timer* by *KISS*. Carl looked at the hacksaw on the floor sitting in a pool of blood, collecting the low orange light of the living room. He saw the knife in Beth's hand. He saw his only daughter's decapitated head resting on the coffee table. Her body slumped in the corner. Eyes listless and turned to the right, as if she died searching for the hands that murdered her.

"I hate dolls." Beth whispered, as she lashed out with the knife and sliced her husband's throat with it. He choked as blood flowed from the gash.

"I got to request a song, Carl." Beth said. Turning, she walked slowly into the bathroom, dropping the carving knife as her husband slumped over, clutching at the wall, blood pouring from his throat and pattering the floor like scarlet rain. He could hear his wife humming a song as she shoved her hand down the kitchen sink and flipped on the switch for the garbage disposal.

"I can't go home right now." Beth said, as she lay dying in a pool of life lost.

The radio still played.

-SOH-

There were several car accidents reported over the course of the next few days.

One woman was driving her Mercedes Benz down North Boulevard in Rehoboth, when she called in on her cell phone to request *Don't Fear the Reaper* by *Blue Oyster Cult*. When it came on she was smiling, dancing to the music in her seat. It reminded her of her father who died of cancer.

Songs have a way of bringing back memory because, like memory, songs are the ghosts of the past; the spirits of voices and the screams of instruments that are trapped beyond the void.

The woman in the Mercedes arrived at her hairdresser appointment that morning, turned off her car's engine and lit herself on fire. She burned herself and her car right down to their skeletons.

-SOH-

Gilby Wallace watched the morning news while his overweight wife came into the living room in her jumpsuit and sweatband. The fish watched her from the corner aquarium as she turned on her radio and began to workout. Through her routine, her husband tried to look around her to see the television but couldn't. The radio was tuned to that special station.

Her song came on the radio; the one *she* requested. She stopped her routine and just stood there, while her husband screamed at her to get out of his way so he could watch the ball game. She stood staring off into space, and then unexpectedly turned and raced forward, grabbed the small aquarium and raised it over her head then lunged toward her husband. Before she brought it down on him, he looked into her eyes and she knew he was glad to die.

The police found Gilby with glass stuck in his

throat and face. A dead fish in his mouth and another in his open palm. The glass had slashed his throat down to the carotids.

His wife lay on the floor hugging her radio, the station still tuned into 15.7 FM. She too was dead, but still there was a smile on her face. Parts of her pink jump suit were washed to a lighter pink, some areas white. Bleach will do that. She had drunk the whole gallon.

-SOH-

Cowboy Sam Hutton saw what was happening, due to the requested songs he played, on the television. The local news said that in a matter of days over forty people were dead in the area. Car accidents, murders, suicides and even packs of dogs running into the streets after children.

At the crime scenes, the police were puzzled.

That night, Sam Hutton had tried to call the owner of 15.7 The BEACH but couldn't get through.

On the way into work while Cowboy listened to the news, he discovered two things: The accidents happened during the hours he was at work and the bloodshed continued throughout his shift.

He didn't want to go back there. He didn't want to look upon the long walls or feel like he was being watched, or smell the smell the smell of sour dirt.

Sam drove while the sky filled with shape-shifting clouds and his shift, only twenty minutes away, loomed closer. The windy stretch of road toward the radio station seemed to reach out to him like a crooked tongue from a demon's maw.

Time felt like an illusion while at work. In the station, Sam noticed the clock on the wall sometimes went in reverse. He couldn't help but scream sometimes at night. Only a few short weeks in Delaware, and here he was...

Where exactly was he?

"Why don't I leave?" he asked his night reflection in the rearview mirror; only his face stared back at him without an answer. "Why haven't I quit if I'm so scared?"

Because you like the music, Sam heard something in his mind say. *You like the beats, Sam, you like sending out the songs...*

The Chevelle, as white as the moon, pulled into the darkened lane made of crushed seashells that separated the woods from the beach resort. Only a mile away was the section of boardwalk, and the starving seagulls that limited their imagination to candy wrappers and half-chewed hot dogs. Opening the Chevelle's door, Sam stepped out into the dark and saw the small brick building with one window lit up with orange light.

I turned that off last night before I left. Maybe Kara or her sons are here.

The key to the old building slipped into the lock and steel door opened. Sam stepped in with his lunch bag in hand then flipped on the short hallway's overhead lights, which pulsated then stayed bright with an eerie hum accompanying the brightness. Walking toward his cubicle, Sam noted the sign above the arch was shining the words ON AIR—

(NO LIFE)

—as the shadows grew ominous and seemed to follow him. Sam looked around the room then sat down beside a box of newspapers someone had brought in since he had last entered the building.

Sam pushed the box aside momentarily and walked to the far wall where the time clock ticked.

He swiped his card. A faint beep called out to him and made him feel comforted for a few seconds. Returning to his seat as the needle reached nine o' clock, Sam donned his headphones, switched on the programs and let the last song run its course. *Catch Me Now I'm Falling* by *The Kinks.*

Sam took the microphone in his hand.

"Hey hey hey folks, this is the Cowboy wishing you a happy hello in the nine o' clock hour as another night has come out of nowhere."

Sam chuckled, it was false. He imagined someone coming up from behind him in the radio station, holding a carving knife and slashing his throat while he was wearing his headphones, and the only thing his audience would hear was his gurgling screams as he drowned on fresh blood.

"Sorry 'bout that, folks. I had to think for a moment. Long day, what can I say? And I know a lot of you have been under strain from what's been going on in town."

Murders...

"But fear not ladies and germs! I got just the thing to lift those spirits! How about some *Van Halen?*"

Sam switched over to live frequency, just as something came through the radio and his headphones that sounded like a young baby screaming. Sam slid out his chair, stood up and smelled the heavy, horrid scent of death.

You don't believe in ghosts, do you?

"Get out of here!" Cowboy yelled out at the room. Quickly, he looked over near the phone and noticed something in the box of newspaper.

Call Kara Waters and tell her you don't want the job anymore.

"I can't." Sam said. "I can't."

And then strange things start to happen all at once. Something walks in front of Sam's cubicle but "walks" isn't exactly the word a person would use to describe the movement. Then swiftly, something drifts across the radio station floor before blowing out like a curtain. Something with a rotting screaming face. Sam sees nothing except maggots crawling along the floor writhing and twisting in time with his harsh breathing.

"I have to get out of here."

But Sam can't leave. He really doesn't know why, but as terrified as he is, he's intrigued.

Something's holding him here. Looking over in the corner at the reception speaker, he sees blood coming from the lines of the felt cusps, as Van Halen pours from the speakers. The vibrations spit blood across the floor, peppering the walls and desks with it.

The song ended just as the phone rang.

"Hello, thanks for calling 15.7 THE BEACH, this is Cowboy he—"

"Hello Cowboy," the strange voice said. It was terrible and exacting, and Sam could hear something behind the voice.

"Who is this?" Sam asked.

"Layne Wolf here, Cowboy. How are you?"

Sam felt his bowels loosen. Time seemed to be trapped—frozen. He was glued to the terror of a dead man's call.

"You..." was all Sam could say.

"Dead?" Layne said. "Is that what you wanted to say? I'm not dead Sam. I'm alive man...I'm alive in my fans and in my *music.* I'm immortal. As long as you keep playing those songs all of us can keep on going on. If you don't...well, that wouldn't make the owner happy, now would it? You'd end up like me, Sam...*dangling.*"

The phone went dead and Sam shivered in terror. He decided to leave but just as he turned, he saw the dead woman in the bathroom—the one with her teeth floating in the toilet. She was smiling. Even in her smile, Sam could see the light through the back of her throat. She reached behind her and flushed the toilet. Sam looked briefly away toward the box of newspapers, and that's when he noticed the woman's obituary. Beside the picture, the name read Kara Waters.

"Sam." The dead thing spoke. "Sam, keep working. There is so much music people want to hear."

"You're not real." Sam said.

"Neither are you." Kara's ghost whispered. "You drove all the way here to Delaware to live. You know why Sam? Because the music's in your blood, in your soul. But the songs belong to the Devil, and now they belong to everyone who is dying."

"No."

"Sam," it said. "Your music will live on, just like all the other songs out there. They are the ghosts of instruments, of poems, little glimpses of talent that can never be forgotten, Sam." It pointed its skeleton hand out toward the box.

"Don't worry about it when you do it. I've got you doing reruns forever, Sam. Your soul is mine."

"What about your sons?"

But the thing before him only smiled as its eyes went from white to glossy black.

He looked in the box now and saw not his boss's obituary, but a pistol.

"Leave my sons out of this."

"They're dead too, aren't they?" Sam asked.

The thing pointed at the gun.

"Do it, Cowboy." It said. "It's high noon."

Sam stood with the gun shaking as his heart slammed like drums in his chest. This place was haunted, and somehow the songs were killing people. It wasn't possible. Sam placed the gun in his mouth and pulled the trigger, sending his teeth flying across the room like piano keys. He died in a pool of blood, listening to the music from one final request. Demons were singing, and whatever songs played, they played for him.

ABOUT THE AUTHORS

Louise Bohmer:
Louise Bohmer is the author of the novel The Black Act. Her short fiction has appeared in numerous venues including MagusPress.com.

Benjamin Bussey:
Benjamin Bussey is a horror writer and loving husband and father. He lives in the UK.

John Dimes:
John Dimes is the author of White Corpse Hustle: A Guide for the Fledgling Vampire, Intracations, and Rites of a Pretending Tribe. His story "Honey on Night Soaked Rind" appeared in the Magus Press anthology *Other Things Other Places.*

Eric Enck:
Eric Enck is the author of *Devotion*, which is being made into a movie. He lives in Delaware. Raising havoc, probably.

John Edward Lawson:
John Edward Lawson is an accomplished poet and novelist. He is the author of The Last Burn in Hell and Discouraging at Best, as well as the poetry collection The Troublesome Amputee.

Joseph McGee:
Joseph McGee is the author of In the Wake of the Night. A chapbook featuring his story The Reaper will be published by Magus Press in 2008.

Joe McKinney:
Joe McKinney is a homicide detective for the San Antonio Police Department. When he's not solving murders, he spends his time writing horror and mysteries and exploring the Texas Hill Country with his family.

Matt Staggs:
Matt Staggs is the founder and editor of www.Skullring.org. His story "The Green Man of Lowland Little Swamp" appeared in the Magus Press Anthology *Other Things Other Places.*

194